The Cigam Chronicles:

Crimson Current

Best Wishes!

Noël [illegible]

Hardcover ISBN: 978-1-62141-815-3
Paperback ISBN: 978-1-62141-816-0

Published by BookLocker.com, Inc., Bradenton, Florida.

Printed in the United States of America on acid-free paper.

Marzen Family Services
Crimsoncurrent@outlook.com
2012

First Edition

The Cigam Chronicles:

Crimson Current

Noël Marzën

Cover Art by Stephanie Knoll

Acknowledgments

The writing of this book would not have been possible without the support and encouragement of my friends and family. Also, I wouldn't have been able to show the world my writing if it wasn't for my High School English teacher and friend, Mary Brinkman, who convinced me to write this book before anyone else knew this story existed. I also want to thank my editor, Rea Mesinovic, for all of her hard work and endless (but very much appreciated) criticism. Special thanks to Stephanie Knoll for the amazing and brilliant hand painted cover. Thank you to my go-to-girl during the most crucial parts of the book, Kristen Heaverlo. I would like to thank God for leading me down the path to my dreams. I will follow you always.

Chapter 1

THE SUN WAS SETTING when I finally headed home. I was probably late for dinner and mom was going to kill me when she saw me. I pulled into my neighborhood and checked my make-up for any smudges, the same thing I always did every time I headed home. Mom hates it when my make-up is smudged and dark; she says I look like a raccoon. When I looked up from the mirror I noticed smoke rising above a house on my road. Then I noticed flashing lights.

I sped up when I got to my street. I didn't realize which house was on fire until I was a few houses down from my own. My house was on fire. I immediately stopped my car on the side of the road and jumped out, leaving my purse on the seat and the keys in the ignition. My breathing accelerated and a thousand thoughts rushed through my mind. The most important question being, where is my family? Was my mom or my brother, Louis inside?

The smoke filled the street and I gasped for clean air as the smoke filled my lungs, but I just kept getting closer. I needed to find out what was happening. I could just make out the flames pouring from the windows on the top floor like a fierce stream. Horror struck through me like a lightning bolt as my adrenaline pumped through me, my home was completely destroyed. All my belongings and possibly my family were being burnt and charred away. As those thoughts sunk in, I started to wonder aimlessly through the thickening smoke, searching for any sign of my family. The flames from the house were blazing with pure rage. I could feel the heat against my skin intensify as I kept walking closer. The smoke was so thick and acrid I couldn't see where I was going. I staggered along the dewy grass trying to get closer to the house, not sure what I was going to do when I got there. My eyes burned from the haze. They were full of tears from the burning of the smoke and the panic that was building up inside me. The lack of oxygen soon took hold of me and I started to see things. An alien in a yellow suit and large dark mouth came at me. I tried to run past it, but it caught me in its arms and picked me up. I tried to fight it off but I was too weak. It carried me to the flashing lights of its space ship, I tried to fight back, but it was too strong. When we reached the flashing lights, the strange creature laid me down on a high table under the lights. I started to hear a familiar voice. It was Luke.

"Charlotte, thank heavens," my stepfather said as he threw his arms around me. His body trembled as he held me close. Now that I was regaining my oxygen levels, I could see clearer. The alien was a firefighter, who had taken his mask off. He had brought me to an ambulance parked across the street. I slowly sat up and pulled away from Luke. His face was red and puffy.

"Where are mom and Louis?" I asked, my voice didn't sound the same; it was hoarse and burned like I had swallowed the fire. I wanted to cough but I knew if I did I wouldn't be able to stop and my throat would hurt worse. I held back the cough as long as I could.

"Charlotte, honey," Luke started as he took my hands in his. His voice was sad and drained. I had never heard him sound like this before. He has been my stepfather for almost seven years and I had never seen him so upset. That's when I knew I needed to ready myself for what he was about to say. "Louis was taken to the hospital in an ambulance an hour ago. I stayed behind to wait for them to find you and your mom."

"They haven't found mom yet?" I asked with some glimpse of hope. But my hope quickly dissolved as soon as I looked at Luke again. His face was red and he was crying. He was a complete mess; normally he was composed and strict. It was like seeing a different person in front of me.

"They didn't find her in time. She didn't make it Charlotte. They said she was down stairs where the fire started. Louis was upstairs; the flames had just reached him when the firefighters rescued him." He sobbed. I stopped listening when he said my mother's body was brought out. Not her, but what was left. My eyes swelled up more as I rubbed them. Chills ran down my spine as I tried to come back to reality. She can't be gone. I saw her this morning before I left for school. She made me breakfast and packed Louis's lunch. She hugged us before we left. That wasn't even twelve hours ago that I saw her alive. How can she be gone in such a short time? It didn't seem real. Then before I could feel anymore emotions piling up on me my sadness turned to anger.

“No! NO! You're lying. She can't be gone. I'll find her.” I shouted shoving away from Luke. I ran as close to the house as I could before it got too hot for me to move. “MOM! MOM!” I screamed for her. The flames built up higher with every scream of pain within me. I fell to my knees and screamed for her until I was pulled away from the emanating heat. The last thing I remember from that night was a blurry figure carrying me to my neighbor's yard and laying me down in the prickly grass. I was pretty sure it was Luke. He held and rocked me until I fell into unconsciousness.

WHEN MY EYES OPENED early the next afternoon, I was in a hospital bed. I was staring up at the ceiling when the memories of last night started to flood back in. “Mom,” I tried to yell but I could barely make any noise at all. I kept trying. “Mom.” I finally managed to scream, it was the most pitiful scream I have ever heard but it was successful. The person sitting in the chair, which I hadn’t noticed before, started to wake up and moved to my side.

“Charlotte, honey, it's alright.” The almost unfamiliar voice said. “I'll get the nurse.” The man that had left me alone in my room was my father. My real father, David. He lives in Europe somewhere with his new family. I see him once a year during the week of my birthday. He sends me Christmas presents and calls me, but I don't care to talk to him much. I never really had a strong relationship with David. He has always tried to get me to come meet his wife and her two sons, but I have never wanted to. He left my mother and me when I was two and I have never forgiven him. He tells me he tried to get us to come with him, but my mom didn't want to go. My mom tried to tell me he left us to go run a magic kingdom, but once I grew out of that phase and realized it was a lie, I didn't want to trust him anymore. I knew my mom was protecting me from the truth. I never asked, I never wanted to know. And now he was here not only to see if I was alright, but to take me back with him. Since I am still a minor and Luke isn't my real father, David will take me back to live with him. This sucks. I still have one year left of school. My mom was planning my senior pictures and we had started to talk about my graduation party. We were going to take a mother-daughter vacation before I went away to college. None of that is going to happen now. I will never see my mother again. She won't be at my graduation, she won't see Louis start first grade, or see me get married or see Louis graduate. I won't have her around for talks we have about boys and friends. She won't be around to help me make decisions that I can't make on my own. What was I going to do without her? What were Luke and Louis going to do without her? What was I going to do without Luke and Louis?

David came back with the nurse and she checked my vitals and flashed a light down my throat and in my eyes. "You look much better, the doctor is going to come talk to you in a bit and you will be able to go home." The woman smiled at me before leaving the room.

"Charlotte..." David started.

"Where is Louis?" I asked.

"He is in the other room."

"Is he alright?" I asked.

"Yes, he will be fine, Luke is in there also. Why don't you go see them, they are in the room next door. I will fill out your paperwork and let you know when the doctor comes to see you." He said.

"I don't want to go back with you." I said before I left the room. I didn't want him to tell me I had to. "How is he," I asked Luke as I walked into the room. Louis was hooked up to a machine and he was still asleep.

"He is doing well, he has first degree burns on his arms and legs, and his lungs are damaged from the smoke but the doctor said he will be just fine. He might have scars from the burns, but nothing too serious. He can go home in a few days." Luke said. His face was still puffy. He came over and hugged me.

"I don't want to go with him." I said with tears in my eyes. "Do I have to go?" I asked.

"Charlotte, I don't want you to go either, but I can't do anything about it. He is your father and he loves you just as much as Louis and I do. I know it will be hard but you can start over there." He said.

I started to cry again. "I don't want to go. I want to stay with you guys. I don't know him." I sobbed into his shoulder.

"I know. I know." Luke said, stroking my hair.

MY MOTHER'S FUNERAL was to be held on Saturday, so her family could be there. And I would be leaving Monday morning to live with David. I didn't want to. I wanted to stay here with Luke and Louis. They were the only ones who were going through the same situation I was in. And I didn't know David very well. Summer Break would start Friday before I left but my teachers still let me off the hook with my semester tests. They said I had enough stress with everything else going on that they would give me study materials and let me use my books on the tests. I already get good grades, but I liked this advantage.

Saturday morning came and went faster than any other day that whole week. Everyone told me how sorry they were for my "loss". People I didn't know hugged me, and they were crying.

The funeral was the most beautiful and the saddest thing I had ever been to. I watched as the oak casket was wheeled down the aisle in our church. It was covered in a bouquet of mom's favorite flower, white Daises. The whole church smelled of them; they didn't smell the best, but it didn't matter to anyone. I remember looking back at the casket as it was being pushed down the aisle and my grandmother, Anne, caught my eye.

She was wearing a black dress with a funny black hat that was from the forties. It reminded me of all the times I used to go over to her house and play dress up using her hats. One day, mom and I played dress up and had a tea party on the terrace at Grandma Anne's. My mom wore a white dress with large black polka dots; she also wore that black hat. Mother always looked so beautiful in whatever she wore. I thought about that day during most of the funeral service. I knew everything there was to know about my mother, and I already knew what the pastor was going to say about her.

SUNDAY I STAYED with Luke and Louis at my Grandma Anne's house. We played games and talked all night, I woke up early Monday morning and said goodbye to both of them.

"Why do you have to leave, Charlie?" Louis said with a sweet, innocent voice. He was only five years old and didn't understand what was going on.

"I'm going to live with my daddy, but I will come back to see you every chance I can, alright? Don't worry, I'll come back." I tried to explain to him. He looked at me strange when I said my daddy; he looked at Luke with a questionable expression, then it turned sweet and soft.

"Are you going to see mommy?" He asked. It took all of my strength not to cry, my eyes watered and my throat tightened but I swallowed hard and didn't let the tears fall over my lids.

"No honey, we aren't going to see mommy again for a long time. Until we go to heaven. She is watching us though, so you better be good. I'll come visit you when I can."

He looked at me with his big brown eyes and then hugged me with his spaghetti arms, not questioning me anymore. "I love you, Charlie," he said with his angelic voice. "I'm going to miss you."

"I'm going to miss you, too. I love you, Louie." I told him. I hugged Luke and Grandma Anne. It was the worst goodbye I have ever done and I kept the tears in long enough to get into the car without Louis seeing me cry.

THE PLANE RIDE was long and boring. It was a four-hour flight to New York, then we switched planes, and it was an eight-hour flight, which seemed like days. The plane supplied three movies, but they were movies I had already seen. I listened for half of the first movie then fell asleep for an hour. When I awoke, they were between movies, so I watched outside my window for a while, even though I couldn't see anything except the blue sky and big white fluffy clouds. I watched the clouds as they moved and made different shapes. One cloud was shaped as a frog doing ballet, another resembled Goofy without a hat. I watched the clouds until the sun started going down. It was beautiful! The sun was a bright orange color, below the sun, the sky was blue fading up to purple then red and finally orange; the higher I looked, the more colorful the horizon was. I watched until the sun finally disappeared.

"Charlotte, wake up, we're there," David told me. I don't remember when I fell asleep, but I had slept the rest of the plane ride. My eyes were still puffy and heavy from crying so even though I slept, I still felt tired.

"Please tell me you live close to the airport, I can't sit any longer," I complained, trying to get the numbness in my butt to go away. I didn't want to keep crying in front of him. I didn't want to be here but I didn't want him to feel bad or try to talk to me about it. We walked out of the airport right as a man standing before us smiled at David and opened the door of a limo for us. He took David's luggage and my one small bag from us and set them in the trunk as we climbed inside.

"I live about a half hour away from here, but we can walk around for a bit, if you want," David started. "You need new things, anyway. Do you want to go to a few stores before heading home?" The way he said "home" made me cringe. It wasn't my home; my home was back with Luke and Louis. I was hoping this would just be temporary, but I knew I was only hoping. This was my home now, indefinitely, at least until I moved out, or went away to college. I should start looking at colleges close to Louis.

"No, I'm tired from the long flight, and I just want to rest. Do we have time to go tomorrow?" I asked as I pulled my feet in close to me, getting comfortable.

"I have to go back to work tomorrow, but my wife, Marilyn, would be happy to take you wherever you need to go," David answered. I know he wanted me to feel at home, but I didn't want to go shopping with Marilyn. She wasn't going to replace my mother, ever. I knew that's not what his plan was but, I guess I could give her a chance. Trying to be difficult was too much work. I should try to settle in as fast as I can so I can try to become happy again. If I fight it I will end up depressed and miserable and being miserable right now is already giving me a stomach ache.

I had fallen asleep again on the way to the house. I was exhausted from the past week's events and just hadn't been getting enough sleep. I woke up right before we reached the gates of the large vineyard; it was very dark. All I could see was the impression of the house in the distance about a quarter of a mile up the driveway. It was a huge house that had a fountain in the center of the circle driveway. The driveway was lit with old style street lights. I had to admit it was beautiful.

"This is where you live?" I asked a little more awake, impressed by the view. The house itself was twice the size of my old house and the land it sat on.

"You live here now too, Charlotte." David told me. I could feel his eyes looking at me but I didn't take my eyes off the house in the distance. I didn't want him to think I was impressed by his lavish life-style.

The house grew bigger and bigger the closer we got to it. I hope the inside is as nice as the outside I thought to myself. When I got out of the limo, David's wife and their maid greeted us. Marilyn pulled me to her and hugged me. She was a tiny lady, very small and bony. "Hello Charlotte, it's so nice to finally meet you. I'm so sorry for your loss. I know it's going to take a lot to get used to but feel free to explore any room in the house, nothing is off limits here. We want you to feel comfortable here." She turned to David and hugged and kissed him. "Come inside you guys." Marilyn seemed nice; she walked me into the house as the maid took my purse and coat to "my room".

"I know it's late, but do you want me to show you around?" Marilyn asked. She smiled at David, then at me. Marilyn had short straight black hair, and her clothes reminded me of a senator. She wore a beige business suit skirt on the bottom and a deep blue blouse on top, the matching coat must be hanging up somewhere.

"Can we look around tomorrow? I'm tired and I've had a long week. I just… I just want to be left alone for a little while, if that's alright." I told them.

"I understand; I will show you to your room." Marilyn said as she tried to break a smile across her face. I felt a little mad at myself for hurting her feelings, she was trying to be nice and welcoming. I told myself I would be nicer to her tomorrow.

"Here is your room, we spent all weekend preparing it for you, and I hope you like it." Marilyn said, kindly.

"Thank you." I said as I walked in with my little bag of belongings I had in my car.

"Charlotte, I'm glad you're here, but I'm so sorry about your mom. I have heard amazing things about her from your dad." She said as she smiled sweetly. "See you in the morning." She closed the door behind me.

AS DARKNESS FILLED the house and everyone was getting ready for bed, I laid wide-awake in the unfamiliar room. It was uncomfortably quiet. I looked around the room, which was glowing from the moon outside the window. The dead silence faded away as I heard muffled noises coming from a vent in the floor. I got out of bed and lay down by it and listened. It was David and Marilyn talking, but I couldn't understand what they were saying. It sounded like a bunch of mumbling, but I still lay listening, it soothed my loneliness…

"Do you think Charlotte will like it here?" Marilyn asked David.

"I think she will, she just needs some time to get used to the environment and all the new changes. But if she is anything like me she will recover quickly. It is hard for me to be sad about things for long periods of time." David answered.

"She must feel lonely, she just lost her mother and now all she has is you, and she doesn't know you that well… I mean, she has to start over." Marilyn says as they talk back and forth.

"I know. I wish I could have been there for her more. I know she doesn't like it here, but I hope she learns to love it. I hope she warms up fast."

“I'm sure she will. I remember when we first moved out here, you didn’t like it either… it took you two weeks to finally give it a chance, and look… now you love it here.”

“That’s probably because of the features of this old house, like the backyard and the library. Those two things were my favorite aspects of this house. I didn’t like it at first because it was different from the states. This country has grown on me.”

“Did you tell her about...?” Marilyn starts but is quickly cut off.

“No. I'm not sure how to tell her. And she has so much to worry about I don't know how to bring it up. I'll just wait and see how she does here.

“I guess we can only wait and let her move at her own pace.” Marilyn said with a sad tone.

“What's wrong?”

“I want her to like me and I know it’s going to be hard for her being the only women in the house besides myself. I want her to be able to come to me with questions, but I’m afraid she isn’t going to want to, because her mother is the one that was there for her. It must be terrible without her mom.”

“Just be a friend to her and she will love you… just like I do.”

“Do you care if I go with you and Charlotte shopping tomorrow? I want to get to know her a little better and let her get to know me, too. I really want her to be happy here and be as comfortable as possible.”

"Actually, I was hoping you would want to go instead of me. I have an important meeting tomorrow night with the council and I need to get my plans for the new storage unit ready to present to the board after that." David said.

"Thanks honey."

Chapter 2

"CHARLOTTE." MARILYN called to me from outside the door. I had fallen asleep on the floor by the vent. I jumped up and crawled into bed.

"Come in," I called back to her.

"How did you sleep?" She asked with a warm joyful voice. Marilyn wasn't in her business attire but rather in jeans and a t-shirt. She came over and stood by the edge of my bed.

"Fine." I didn't know what else to say. We were in awkward silence for a few seconds until Marilyn broke in.

"Umh, your dad is busy working on some business, and asked me to take you to get some more clothes, and maybe a few things to make you feel more comfortable here. Is that alright?"

"Yeah, I guess that's fine."

A small smile formed on Marilyn's face as she said, "Okay, well why don't you get dressed and come down for breakfast and we can leave after that."

Breakfast was good; David had his own chef, which didn't surprise me after the maid took my purse last night when I arrived. Chef Mallow was a very sweet man; he whipped up anything I asked for, which wasn't much since I didn't have my appetite fully back to normal from my exhausting misadventure.

"Thank you for the breakfast it was very good." I complimented then asked. "Where is Marilyn?"

"You're welcome." Chef Mallow said, "I think Ms. Marilyn is in her office, it's the second door on the left, off the living room."

"Thank you." I said as I gave him a smile and walked towards the living room. The living room was all white and seemed kind of small compared to the rest of the house; it was smaller than the room I was staying in.

(Knock, Knock)

"Come in," Marilyn told me. I walked into the small room; Marilyn was sitting at a large brown desk, talking on the phone. She motioned me to take a seat in front of the desk where two chairs were present. "Alright, yeah, that sounds great… Yep, can't wait to see you too, I will call you tomorrow. Okay, love you." She hung up the phone and smiled at me.

"That was my son Harper, he finished school a week ago and is at a camp working all summer but he will be back two weeks before school starts. He's your age." She paused for a brief second and continued when I didn't say anything. "So, did you get enough to eat?"

"Yes."

"Good, let me grab my purse and we can go."

THE SHOPPING TRIP went pretty well. Marilyn seemed sincerely interested in what I liked. I wasn't exactly thrilled at shopping but I wasn't sure how much longer I would want to wear the same outfit. The first thing we went to get me was a cell phone, which hadn't even crossed my mind for something to get, but then Marilyn said if I didn't want to shop with her she would understand and all I had to do was call her when I was done. I know she was just giving me space if I wanted it, but I couldn't be mean to her, plus I didn't want to be left alone. After spending three short hours of buying clothes, we went out for lunch. I was starting to like Marilyn; she was genuine and very open when she talked. She didn't hold anything back, if she didn't like something she told me. And when I wanted to talk she just listened, she only gave her opinion when I wanted it, which was nice to just be able to talk and have someone not tell me what they think, but to just listen and let me get all my thoughts out. I was so comfortable talking to Marilyn that I shared stories about my mom and the good old days we had shopping together. I wasn't sure if that would upset Marilyn until after I had started to talk about it, but I looked for any change in her face, but found only smiles. She even told me some stories of her own. I was really grateful I came shopping today with Marilyn and not David; because I'm sure this experience would not have been the same and I might not have seen this side of Marilyn right away. I feel like I made a friend today that I didn't know I could have.

"CHARLOTTE WOULD YOU like to come to work with me today?" David asked me during breakfast. The only part of the vineyard I had seen was the grape vines I could see from my bedroom window. I don't drink, so wine isn't very appealing to me and I wasn't thrilled about looking at or learning about it, but I didn't want to disappoint David. He was just trying to get me out of the house.

"That sounds like it could be fun." I smiled at him before I took another bite of my toast.

David owned a large vineyard and winery where he grew grapes, strawberries, and raspberries, for making juice, jam, and, of course, wine. The whole wine making process was done in the buildings surrounding the fruit, the only time any products left the vineyard was when they were completed and ready to be sold.

"We planted apple, pear, and cherry trees a few years ago, so we could try them as wine also." David informed me as we walked along the path to the vineyard about a quarter mile up from the house. There were many workers picking unripe grapes in the field next to us. I watched as I wondered what they were doing. David saw my curiosity.

"This is the green harvest. They are picking bunches of grapes to limit the weight the vines have to support. This delivers more nutrients to the remaining grapes and also gives them a richer flavor." David informed me. When we arrived at the three large buildings at the end of the path, the sun was going behind the house. It reminded me of the sunset I saw on the plane. It had the same bright colors and the same color clouds. I couldn't help but let my mind drift to my mother. I missed her so much. I wondered what we would be doing right now if she was still here. Would we be playing ball outside with Louis? Or maybe we would be swimming at the lake. Or maybe we would be baking cookies. I felt a tear escape from the corner of my eye and run down my cheek. I quickly wiped it off and followed David inside.

Even with the light on, it was still dark. The whole place smelled like grape juice. David led me to the first part of my tour, the beginning of the wine making process. We walked through each step as we moved throughout the building. When we came to the end of the process we entered another room. It was full of wine racks and large jugs and barrels labeled with times and dates when each was made. Most of them were from last year's harvest but some were anywhere from two to eight years.

"This barrel is part of the first batch I ever made." David told me as he pointed to a barrel in the back of the room. It looked much older than all of the rest and the date was from 2004.

"How did you know you wanted to start a winery?" I asked him. He took a few minutes to answer, while he walked over to the wine rack.

"This vineyard was Marilyn's families, and when we married, the family handed it down to her, but she wasn't as interested in it as much as her other family had been, so she wanted to sell it, but I wouldn't let her. Since then on, I have been running it. Sometimes people don't choose to do things, those things choose them." David explained. "This bottle," he started as he pulled on the cork until it popped open, "is white grape and strawberry wine. It is my favorite." He pulled out two glasses from a shelf next to the wine rack. "Would you like to try it?" I nodded and he handed me a glass. My first instinct was to smell it. It was the same sweet smell that the whole building had. I tipped the glass letting the pink wine barely touch my lips. The taste was sweet but also had a tingle to it that I guessed most alcohol probably had. It was good though. I took an actual drink this time. "Do you like it?"

"It is different, but yeah it's good." I said. I liked the wine but not enough to want more. Even if the drinking age in Europe was lower than it was in the U.S., I still didn't mind waiting until I was 21. After David cleaned out the glasses and returned them to the place he got them, he grabbed the bottle of wine he had opened and we walked back up to the house. It was dark outside but the path was lit by vintage green street lamps. I hadn't noticed them before now, but I hadn't been here long enough to notice much. The fruit trees were lit up by Christmas lights, also. "Won't that hurt the trees, having those lights on it?"

"No, they are fine." David answered with a smile. "I had fun with you Charlie. I really hope you can make yourself at home here. It was terrible what happened, but I'm very glad you are alright and I get a chance to get to know you."

"Thanks, David- uh, Dad. It is nice here. I just need some time to get used to things. It's just not the same and it never will be." I tried to hold back my tears. I missed my mom so much. She would have loved to see this place.

"Charlie, you know if you ever need anything or anyone to talk to, both Marilyn and I are here for you."

"I know, I just can't believe I will never see her again. I never even got to say goodbye." I said as tears finally broke free from my eyes and fell to my cheeks. David pulled me close to his side.

“I know it’s hard without her, and it will be hard for a while. Time can only make it better.” He said as he kissed my head.

“I just miss her so much.” I bawled.

Dear Luke and Louis,

How are you guys doing? I miss you both so much. I feel like I have been gone forever. I hope to see you soon. Have Louis call me anytime he needs something, I would love to talk to him. I miss you and I love you

Charlotte

I have really gotten used to it here. I spend a lot of time in the library, typing. I send messages to Luke and Louis, sometimes as much as six times a day. I haven’t gotten the courage to explore yet. This house is huge, and the yard is even bigger. I have made friends with Chef Mallow, he is pretty cool. He lets me help him cook sometimes and he tells me lots of stories about Marilyn and her boys, Harper and Kaisen. Harper will be turning 18 six months after I do. Kaisen turns 19 a few months after my birthday. So we are all very close in age. I will be meeting Harper at the end of the summer before we start our senior year of high school. Kaisen is taking summer classes at his college so I won't meet him until Thanksgiving. Summer is turning out to be fairly good, considering the circumstances. I get to call Louis whenever I want and I can Skype with my friend Holly from back home, and no one brings up my mother, which makes it a lot easier not to think about the fire.

I am a lot more like David than I realized. We have some of the same habits, for instance we both eat macaroni and cheese with ketchup. Marilyn thinks we are both weird when it comes to eating habits. I have David's nose, chin and cheek bones. I also have his dark brown hair and the same argument strategy. For living so far away for so long we seem to have the same reaction to almost everything, which makes me wonder: am I the sophisticated one or is he the immature one?

"Charlotte, may I come in?" David asked, as he cracked my door open waiting for my response.

"Yeah," I answered. I had woken up early and was lying down on my bed with a book. I sat up as David entered my room.

"I have a business meeting outside of Paris and Marilyn will be gone all afternoon, are you all right to stay here by yourself?"

"I'll be fine here; won't Chef Mallow be here as well as the other staff?"

"Yes, they'll be here, but they will be working."

"Then I'll be fine. Besides I have the library to entertain me."

"Well we won't be too long; we should both be back before dinner." He came over and kissed my forehead before he left.

I waited until I couldn't hear him in the hall; I got dressed and went down stairs to get breakfast from Chef Mallow.

"What are you going to do this morning, Ms. Charlotte?" Chef Mallow asked. He always called people by a proper name.

"Do you have to call me Ms. Charlotte? It sounds… funny." I asked in a smile.

"What would you like me to call you, ma'am?" He asked, partially sarcastic. Chef Mallow was funny and very nice. He was a heavy man which made it easy to remember his name because he resembled a Marshmallow.

"I don't know, anything but Ms. Charlotte. That sounds like a name of a ship."

"All right," he said pausing for a moment, acting like he was thinking of an appropriate nickname. "How about… Chuck?"

"No," I laughed.

"Charlie?"

"Charlie? My little brother calls me that." I agreed.

"Well then, Princess Charlie, what would you like to eat?"

I cringed when he said "princess," I gave him a jokingly dirty look, and shrugged him off. "How about some breakfast pizza?" I asked him. Before I could say any more he had a medium sized breakfast pizza in front of me.

"I knew that's what you would want. So… you never did answer my question. What are you going to do this morning?"

"I haven't decided, but I think I'm going to explore the house, I have only seen a few rooms and I want to look around a bit."

"Have fun with that, but don't explore the maze without anyone to go with you. When Kaisen and Harper where younger, they raced through the maze and Kaisen got lost and it took Marilyn two hours to find him." Chef Mallow was being serious but let out a small laugh at the same time.

"I thought they just moved here, when Marilyn and David got married?"

"Marilyn and the boys have lived here since Harper was born, but David moved in after they got married. This was Marilyn's family's vineyard and she had already been running it when they met."

"Oh, I just assumed they moved here together to take over the vineyard after the wedding. Well, thanks for the breakfast, but if it's okay I'm going to take a few pieces to go." I said with a smile, and then strolled out of the kitchen.

I walked around the house for a couple hours, just looking at the different rooms. There had to be at least thirty. I noticed that down the hall from my room was Kaisen's. Across from his room was Harper's room. There were three other doors in this hallway. The door next to mine was a bowling alley with four lanes, the door across from that was a home theater system equipped with a popcorn machine and a mini bar filled with candy and pop. All the way down the hall, next to Harper's room, was the last door. It was very dark inside because there weren't any windows. I wasn't sure what this room was for until I took a trip inside. I searched for a light switch with my fingers blindly running along the walls. I found a small round switch… I turned it. The lights faded up, it was a huge room with black walls with long vertical slits. There was a large keyboard on the wall next to the light switch. I walked over to it. I pressed a green button that read "power." A screen I hadn't noticed at first lit up above the keyboard. It had a bunch of titles on it… Tropical Paradise, Alien Planet, Jungle, Appalachian Mountains… I was curious, and a little confused so I pressed the button that read "Tropical Paradise." Instantly, the black walls changed into a beach scene with palm trees and where the slits in the wall were, large palm trees lit up. What was this place, I thought to myself… I wasn't sure, but it was pretty cool. It must have been a virtual reality system. I pressed Appalachian Mountains next… it got colder instantly, the scenery was mostly gray mountains and rock formations. The tropical trees faded into snow caps and the long beach was now a snowy ledge. It was beautiful and so surreal. After playing with the room's virtual system, I turned it off and kept exploring.

FOR THE NEXT FEW weeks I did the same thing almost every day. I read in my room, typed to friends and family on the computer and ate meals when I was supposed to. I moped around the house when I was too upset to read or talk to anyone. I just couldn't pull myself together some days. I was on the verge of a major breakdown when Marilyn came up to talk to me. She always tried to cheer me up, with little success.

"Charlotte, may I come in?" She asked as she stood outside my bedroom door.

"I don't care." I called from in my pillow. I had been crying all day and my eyes and nose were red and sore from rubbing them. I hadn't changed from my pajamas, even though it was four o'clock in the afternoon.

"Sweetie, are you alright?" She asked as she sat next to me on the bed. She rubbed my back and didn't let me respond to her question. "Hon, your father and I are worried about you. I know you are still upset about your mom, but you need to know that she wouldn't want you to put yourself through this, would she? Even though she isn't here with you now, doesn't mean you should forget about her but you need to keep going. She would want you to be strong and be happy again. This is your chance to start over and I know you might not want to but will you please try? Your father loves you so much and we all hate seeing you like this." She paused to see if I was still listening. I didn't know what to do; I knew she was right even if I didn't want her to be. And no matter how hard I think it is, I needed to be happy. I need to forget about the bad stuff that happened, but not forget my mother. I wiped my face on my pillow before I sat up to hug Marilyn.

"I'm sorry." I apologized.

Chapter 3

Dear Luke,

How are you? I'm fine. I found some pictures of mom today. They are really old but I wasn't sure if you found anything of hers in the fire. I miss her so much. I miss you both so much too. I scanned the pictures to the computer and am sending them to you. Tell Louis I love and miss him, and I can't wait to see him. I love you and miss you, too.

Charlotte

TWO MONTHS AGO, I was hanging out with friends and still had my mom around to help me with school and work. She was still in my life… physically. Now I am in the process of starting a new life with my dad and his new family. My mother is still a big part of my life, but only in the mental images that will be preserved in my mind forever. I have been through a lot these past few months but my dad and his wife have made it easier than it should ever be. I feel like I have known them a long time and wish, now, that I had them in my life before I was forced by law to live with them.

I have decided to let go of the hurt in my past and let my new life take its place. I will never forget my mother or my friends and family I left behind when I came to Europe. I am letting go of the fire and my old belongings and not looking at the bad in it all, but instead looking at it in a different perspective. Everything happens for a reason, even if it was hard to comprehend. I was supposed to live with my father, maybe if I would have given him a chance my mother would still be here, maybe not. I didn't know the reason for this disaster, but I know in my heart everything will be all right.

I had already given this place a chance and to my surprise, I actually liked it. If I had to live anywhere besides with Luke and Louis, it would be here. David was the nicest businessman I had ever met. He owned one of the largest vineyards in Europe and was the head of command. He was caring and loving and tried to make time for his family. I wasn't fond of his wife Marilyn when I first met her. She seemed too cheery, almost fake. She had actually turned out to be a very nice lady. She wasn't old, or boring, she liked the same things I did, so all in all, she was cool. I will meet Harper, Marilyn's youngest son today. I'm sure if I like his mother, I will like him, too. If I don't I will get over it, eventually.

I walked down the hallway from my room and entered into the library. The library was the best room in the house. It reminded me of the library in 'The Beauty and the Beast.' The library was two stories. When I walked in I was standing on the top floor. There was a balcony with matching staircases on either side. Books lined the walls. Under the balcony were double doors that led me down a long corridor. This led to the main hallway, where the master bedroom was, along with Marilyn and David's offices, and other unknown rooms.

Marilyn went with Tom, the chauffeur, shopping and to pick up Harper from the airport. I walked down the grand staircase, passing the living room where David was sitting with some associates from his company. Before I could fully pass the meeting, David stopped me for an introduction.

"Good morning, Charlotte." David started, "Gentlemen, this is my daughter."

"Nice to meet you all," I said politely. I smiled as they all stood to greet me. "I'm going to explore the maze after breakfast if that's alright?"

"Take your phone with you and call me if you need anything at all. I will be done shortly."

"Okay." I walked passed them out of the living room and into the kitchen to see what Chef Mallow was cooking for breakfast.

"Chef Mallow, I hope you have a big breakfast made, I'm starving." I said jokingly as I smiled.

"How do fried donuts sound? I also made pancakes." He answered.

"Sounds good to me, I'll have fried donuts." I said. "What are you making for lunch?"

"We will have a small lunch today," he started, "Mr. Harper won't be back until supper time so I'm making it big. Ms. Marilyn won't be here for lunch either so it will just be you and Mr. David. We are having sandwiches for lunch and Mallow Roast for dinner. It is my own special recipe."

"Thanks for the breakfast, it was wonderful. I'm going to go exploring again. Please call me for lunch when it's ready." I said after eating and putting my plate away.

"Yes, your majesty," he said with a grin. I just gave him a joking glare and walked out of the room.

All right, there is a trick to this maze, I thought to myself as I walked out into the sunny yard. *I just have to find out what it is.*

The maze was about a half mile in length. I had time to spare so I took a deep breath and headed in. Right when I got inside the hedge, I had to turn right; the path wouldn't let me go anywhere else. I walked about twenty feet and I had to turn almost all the way around to stay on the path. I walked about ten feet and came to another one way. So, I turned right and kept heading down the path. I thought the maze was really easy to get through; everywhere I went was a one way. How can anyone get lost if the whole maze is like this?

I kept walking when I came to the first T-intersection. I looked down both paths and they both looked the same, green hedges on both sides and a brown dirt path on the ground. I turned left and walked down a short path that led me to another left. I turned and looked down that path and there was a large mirror hanging on the maze wall not far from where I was standing. This scared me because I saw myself but at a quick glance I thought I saw someone else and my heart jumped into my stomach as I gasped. I looked closer at it and laughed. It was a dead end, so I turned back and took the other direction. I walked on through the maze running into T-intersections and more dead ends. I walked for about ten minutes when I came to a fork in the path. This was a three-way intersection. I took the middle path; I met another intersection followed by another until finally I came to a dead end. I turned back and took the other direction from the last intersection. That also came to a dead end. This was confusing. Neither path was correct, I had to go back to the intersection before this one and start again. Neither of those paths led on either, they all came to dead ends. I walked back and forth trying to find my way when I walked all the way back to the fork intersection. I took the path on the left this time, but eventually I was lead back to the fork intersection.

All right, I have to take the path on the right, I thought. I walked down a few paths again and hit a few dead ends, until I came to an intersection that had signs above each path. The one on the left said 'the long way' and the right one said 'the short cut.' *Was this a trick,* I asked myself, *which way should I take?* If I hit a dead end I can always come back and take the other direction.

I took the short cut; it took me to where the path ended and where a big area was. It had three white park style benches in a circle around a large circle gazebo. The gazebo was white and had icicle lights hanging down from the ceiling; it had a brown wood dance floor. There was music playing but I had to really listen to hear it. This garden-like area had flowers around the outside of the gazebo and when you look up at the sky, there are lights hanging across the top of the hedges, so when it's dark they light up the whole area. I must be in the center of the maze, that didn't take very long. David said it takes hours to get through the whole thing, and he is the only one who has ever made it through the whole thing the first time. Usually when people go through the maze they get lost or can't make it through in one try. I looked down at my phone. Oh. I was in here a lot longer than I thought. If I'm already half way through it, it will take me another two hours to get out. There were two paths at the opposite end of the garden. I went down the left one this time and walked a long ways but there were no more intersections or dead ends. I kept walking until finally I came to another open area. But it looked like the same garden I was just at. It was the same garden. I had just walked in a circle.

I picked up my phone and called David.

"David- Dad, I am in the maze and I can't find my way out, will you come help me?" I said hoping he wasn't busy.

I could hear him laugh, "Sure, give me ten minutes to find you, do you know what side of the maze you are on?"

"I'm in an open area with a gazebo and Christmas lights." I explained.

"You got far; I know exactly where you are. I will see you soon, stay there."

It's going to take him more than ten minutes to get here, it took me two hours to make it this far. I wonder if he has a map to the maze, or maybe he knew it well enough to take the correct turns.

I sat down on one of the benches and waited for David to get there. I waited and watched the pathway that led me here.

"Come on, I'll show you the trick to get out of here," David said as he came up behind me.

"You scared me, how did you get here? I watched the entrance to the garden and you didn't come from that way."

"I came from the secret passage from the yard to this garden. There are many hidden pathways to get here but you have to look for them. Since you got lost and have already found this garden I'll show you the passage out of here, in case you get stuck again." David said as he smiled at me. He led me to the hedge wall that had a single red leaf on it, barely visible, even up close. It was just at eye level and smaller than all the rest of the leaves.

David reached his hand out to the small red leaf and stuck it through the hedge right underneath of it so it was barely touching his arm. I watched in excitement as the hedge opened to a pathway.

"If you use these passages, you must close the door behind you." He said in a serious voice.

"Okay, I will," I said in excitement. He led me down the narrow pathway as we came to a hedge wall, I looked around, and there was no way out. I looked at the hedge in front of me, and there, barely visible, was a small red leaf. "Is that another opening?" I asked as David nodded. "Can I try?" I reached out my hand and put it in the hedge just below the red leaf and felt around. There was a handle with a small lever on it; I pulled the lever and a door opened to just outside the maze.

"Whoa, that was really neat." I said.

"I'm glad you like it, I like to escape sometimes, and the trap doors come in handy when trying to get out in a hurry or just too lazy to try to find the real exit. I think I have only used the exit twice." He smiled.

"Thanks for showing me."

"No problem, just make sure you take your phone every time you go into the maze. Just because there are ways out does not mean you can always find them and some of them have been known to get stuck shut. And make sure you always tell someone you are going in there, so if something happens we know where to find you." He was being very serious now.

"I will."

"You must be hungry. Do you want to go out for lunch?"

"Sure."

"Okay, go up and change, we will leave as soon as you're ready."

THE REST OF THE DAY went by very fast; when David and I got back from lunch, I went back up to my room, stopping at the library for a book first. I didn't like reading that much but since I have been here that is about all I have done. I had been reading a series of books before I came here and I was curious on what happened in them. When I found them in the library, I had to pick them up and read the rest of them. I read for a few hours, it was easy for me to lose track of time in my books when I had something interesting to read. I mostly enjoyed romance novels and fantasy books. When I found a series with both romance and fantasy in it, I fell in love with them. I had just ended a chapter when David knocked on my door. He told me that his parents were coming for dinner and they would be here in an hour. I need to get ready. I was supposed to wear something nice. Marilyn and Harper would be back a little after my grandparents. I told him that I would get ready after I went downstairs to get something to drink. He nodded at me and left the room quietly.

On my way back up to my room, I walked past the virtual reality room. I still hadn't found out what the rooms intent was. I thought for a while about this room, was I missing something? I pondered over the mystery of the room for a few minutes, and then noticed I was staring off into space. I quickly re-gathered my thoughts and walked into my room. My room was wonderful, way better than what my room had looked like in America. This room was my favorite color…pink. It was a lot of pink, maybe even too much, but I liked it. The carpet was a light pink shade that blended well with the walls, which were also pink, but in a textured look. When I walked into my room the first thing in my view, and closest to me was a small round table. The table was made of some kind of dark stained wood. The table was small and round with a bowl of pink potpourri, for decoration, in the middle. Next to the table, on the opposite side of where I was standing was a pink chaise with matching pink pillow. The chaise was facing a flat screen television that hung from the ceiling. It could be seen from the chair and the bed, which was sitting on the right side of the room, in the middle against the wall. The bed was a light pink with gold tassels and accents. The headboard was a pale gold-yellow. Above the bed was a crystal-based chandelier that somehow did not block the television. There were matching bedside tables on each side of the bed. Matching pink lamps sat on each of them, also. The whole bed looked like it was from the Victorian Era. The bed was double, with huge pillows that took up most of the space. There were three windows on the far wall. One parallel to the bed, one a little farther than the television, and one parallel to the vanity which was stained to match the rest of the wood tables in the room. It had a large round mirror in the center. At the far end of the extravagant room, across from the bed, was a double door closet. The doors had hanging racks for my belts and purses. On the left side of the closet were shelves and drawers. It carried everything that couldn't be hung up. On the right side was everything else… everything that could be hung up. Even though I had only been shopping once, my closet was completely full. Marilyn had given me some of her clothes and she was a shop-aholic. The day she took me shopping was the largest shopping trip of my life. She took me into thirteen different stores and we didn't walk out of a single store without buying at least two bags full of stuff. It wasn't just clothes either; we bought handbags, jewelry, room accents, accessories, body lotions, even towels matching my room had the name...Charlotte hand sewn on. In one day worth of shopping, we probably spent close to eight thousand dollars. We went out to eat at a Tapas Bar for lunch. It was the most amazing shopping day ever. We walked several miles and also road in a large taxi.

As I dreamed about my first day here and how my room looked, I heard a noise coming from down the stairs. People were talking. I walked down the long corridor to see who was here. It was an old couple; they were hugging David and taking off their coats. Did I really lose track of time? Was that David's parents? I was supposed to be getting ready for our dinner guests and I forgot all about it. I rushed back to my room, throwing my closet door open searching for something to wear.

I put on an outfit that was hanging together in my closet; it was almost like it was waiting for me. The whole outfit was ready to go. It was a knee length black pencil skirt with a silver shirt with a red cardigan. Below the hanging outfit was a pair of silver pumps. Around the neck of the hanger that the outfit was hanging from, were a set of three colored beaded bracelets and a matching necklace. I put on the outfit and curled the ends of my hair pulling up the sides in an invisible sized rubber band. I put on makeup and rushed out the door. I walked very fast but as elegant as I could, I wanted to make a good first impression. I walked down one side of the grand staircase and into the sitting area where David was. As they noticed that I was entering the room, David and his parents stood to greet me.

"Charlotte, these are my parents and your grandparents, Charles and Gretta." David said introducing me.

"Nice to meet you both." I told them as I gave them both a hug.

"It's very nice to finally meet you, my child. We have been looking forward to this since you were born." Gretta said in a scratchy voice. She was short and thin with silver hair that was wrapped in a bun on the upper part of her head. She didn't look like a grandma, apart from the hair; she had semi-smooth skin. Her skin wasn't wrinkly like normal old ladies, and her husband didn't look very aged either. He looked like he was David's much older brother but too young looking for his father or my grandfather for that matter. They were nice people, and I supposed that sooner or later I would have to start calling them grandma and grandpa but it was nice that they didn't seem that way. I am not fond of old people, especially the really old kind.

Old people smell funny and did weird things and sometimes don't see or hear well. These old people were different though, I wondered if it was a genetic thing or if they had plastic surgery. That was common around here; everyone in Paris looked fake, so beautiful it didn't look real.

"Do you like it here, Charlotte?" Charles asked.

"Yes, it's very nice."

"Well, I'm glad you like it. We are glad to have you here." He added. We sat in an awkward silence for a few minutes until there was a small flash of light through one of the windows facing the driveway.

"Ah, Marilyn and Harper are here, finally." David said jumping up and rushing to the door. I did the same. The silence was deafening and uncomfortable. It was almost like David's parents could hear what I was thinking or at least could hear what each other where thinking. They looked back and forth at each other like they were having a mind-to-mind conversation. It was kind of creepy.

Chapter 4

DAVID OPENED THE DOOR for Marilyn and Harper as they walked into the house. The wind blew inside and it was warmer outside then it was inside. It was sticky and warm, like the beach almost.

"How was your flight?" David asked a handsome young man who walked into the large open door.

"It was boring and long, until I got off and thought everyone forgot about me." Harper said in smooth, deep voice. He gave Marilyn a glare but couldn't hold it for more than a few seconds when a little smirk rose to his lips. Harper was tall and muscular. He had dark hair like Marilyn and had her smile. He was so cute. He looked much older than 17.

"I couldn't find the terminal, the man at one of the desks said 76A not 67A." Marilyn said in a small voice with her head down as she talked to David, then turned to the boy and said, "I already said I was sorry a million times. Will you ever forgive me?"

The young man grinned, "I'm just joking... Of course I forgive you."

Marilyn gave him a loving smile and turned to look at me. "Oh... Harper this is Charlotte, David's daughter, the one I was telling you about." She explained as if he wasn't able to comprehend the first part.

"I guessed that." he said to Marilyn, then turning to me, greeting me with a quick hand squeeze. It couldn't be a handshake because it was just a brisk grab of the hand then he let go. "Nice to meet you, Charlotte. I'm Harper."

"Nice to meet you, too." I said. I was so glad he was good looking. That would make it easier for me to get along with him. When he dropped my hand, I felt instantly warmer. It was a weird feeling, but I liked it. Harper was very, very good looking, not that I wanted to... like him like that.

David's cell phone rang.

"Hello?" David answered. "Oh, hello..." He started but then was cut off by the person on the other end of the line. I noticed he took a short glance at Marilyn, and then walked off into the other room, where he couldn't be heard.

"Shall we go into the living room and wait to be called to dinner?" Marilyn asked in a rhetorical question to get everyone out of the entryway. As the grandparents greeted Marilyn and Harper, we walked into the living room.

"I see you found the outfit I picked out for you." Marilyn said with a mischievous grin.

"Yes, thank you." I said.

We talked for a while until David entered back into the room.

"Who was that on the phone?" Marilyn asked.

"It was nothing." He said. David isn't a very good liar, at least in the short amount of time I had been here; I could tell when he wasn't telling the whole truth. I wondered who he was talking to on the phone, whoever it was; he was trying to keep it a secret from Marilyn. I wasn't psychic or anything but I understood the way he looked at her.

"So are we ready for dinner then?" Marilyn asked, oblivious to his lie.

"No. Not yet, I don’t think Chef Mallow is done. Be patient he will call us when it is ready." He said in a more calming tone. I could tell this was part of the lie. Were they making something special for Marilyn? Or... was someone coming for dinner she didn't know about? Maybe I was wrong but something was up.

We waited in the living room talking for another ten to twenty minutes before I heard a strange noise. The sound of a car in the driveway or...

Chef Mallow came into the living room, "Dinner is served." he said out of breath and startled. It was odd.

We walked into the dining room slowly but surely. David got another call on his cell, that, this time, he kept in the room and talked to someone right in front of us... "Yes? Now? We are getting ready for dinner... Sure. I will be right there." He said hanging up the phone.

"Don't tell me that was a work call?" Marilyn asked.

"Someone is here." He said with a half grin, which you could tell he was trying to sustain it from her eyes. He turned swiftly towards the front door, which was visible from the dining room. There was a loud knock at the door right as he reached for the door handle. This was too obvious, it was easily noticed that the whole scene was planned out.

David reached for the door, cracking it open just enough that Marilyn couldn't see, as he looked to see if she was looking, which she wasn't. "Oh darling, the door is for you...," he said revealing his big grin and the unexpected guest at the door, at the same time. Marilyn glanced up with a confused expression, until she saw the surprise at the door. My breath caught when I saw the young man standing in the doorway with a big grin on his face as well. Marilyn jumped to her feet and ran to the door, hugging the man. It must be Kaisen. I have seen pictures but he looks different in person. He looked just like Harper, but with a little bit of facial hair, and even more gorgeous. He was more muscular than Harper. They were the same height and had the same dark hair. His smile was different from Harper's though. It must come from his father. Kaisen was so beautiful he could pass as a model. There was something about him that made me feel nervous and anxious at the same time.

"Oh my god, I can't believe you're home. I have missed you so much, Kaisen." Marilyn exclaimed with joy. "I thought that you wouldn't be able to get a break until Thanksgiving?"

"I got done with some finals early. I can only stay for a few days. David and I planned to surprise you so Harper and I could be here at the same time." Kaisen explained.

"This is the best surprise ever. Oh, we have someone we would like you to meet..." She said remembering that I was here. "This is Charlotte, David's daughter. She has come to live with us." She was excited to show me off, which was weird because I had only been here and known her for a short time. Maybe she was just excited that Kaisen came home early... I couldn't tell.

"Nice to meet you, Charlotte." Kaisen said. His enthusiastic grin turned into a charming smile that made me want to melt when he looked at me. I smiled back.

"Nice to meet you, too." I told him as he reached to shake my hand, I reached for his too. Instead of a quick grasp like Harper, he reached down and kissed my hand. It was weird but I loved every second of it. My stomach jumped when his lips touched my skin. I couldn't help to think about meeting Harper a few minutes ago, who felt like a stepbrother type and felt weird thinking he was cute, but Kaisen was a-whole-nother story. Maybe it was just a first impression thing. Hopefully he would get on my nerves and let me not think of him that way... even if he was handsome.

I never would have thought Marilyn's boys would be so charming. They are the total opposite when it came to personalities but are exactly the same when it came to most of their adorable features. Their smiles made a warming feeling inside me, as well as the way they spoke. I thought about this for a while as everyone else ate their dinner and talked. After dinner we all sat around in the living room talking and catching up. It was surprisingly easy to talk to Harper and Kaisen. Usually it's hard to talk to boys, especially the cute ones. I giggled at myself when I thought about that. Luckily, no one heard me.

David's parents were very nice people. As they left, they hugged me and were very kind. Gretta slipped a small jewel covered square box into my hand and whispered, "This is for you, my child." She kissed me on the forehead, said goodbye and left.

I held the box in my fist so no one else could see the tiny gift.

"It's getting late; you guys should probably head upstairs to your rooms." Marilyn told us.

"It's only 10:30." Harper complained.

"I didn't say you had to go to bed I said you had to go to your rooms. But, I'm tired, and I'm going to bed. I don't care if you stay up just don't wake me up." She said with a wink that was directed at me.

"Alright, good night mother." Harper said, a little more cheerful. He kissed her goodnight, as did Kaisen and they walked slowly away.

"Goodnight, Marilyn." I said as I hugged her.

"Goodnight, Charlotte, I will see you in the morning." She said, kissed my forehead and walked towards her bedroom on the opposite side of the house.

I hid the box in my hand until I got to my room. I sat on my bed and gazed at the little gold box covered in different colored gems. I opened up the container and found an emerald ring inside with a silver and gold twisted band. It was absolutely beautiful; I tried it on right away. It fit perfectly on the ring finger on my right hand.

As I lay in bed idolizing my new ring, I could hear laughter coming from down the hallway. I wonder how long it's been since Kaisen and Harper have seen each other. Marilyn had mentioned Kaisen's college ran long and he doesn't usually have a break except for during Holidays. That must really suck, only seeing family once or twice a year. I wonder what college he goes to and how far away it is; maybe I'll ask him tomorrow. As I thought about the boys laughing in the other room, I shortly drifted to sleep.

Chapter 5

KAISEN KNOCKED ON my door right before breakfast.

"I'm only home for the rest of this week, so Harper and I made plans to go to Grufon Dunes with some friends. Do you want to come with?" Kaisen asked politely.

"Umh… sure, that sounds cool." I said with a smile. That sounds cool? What am I twelve, I can't find a better word than cool? I'm so dumb.

"Okay, good." He said with a weird look. By the look on his face, it seemed like he was about to say something else but he held his tongue. He just smiled and left my room.

"Harper, hurry up. We are going to Grufon Dunes when you get done with breakfast." Kaisen said.

"That sounds like fun. Do you care if Charlotte goes with you boys? I think she would enjoy that. You could introduce her to some of your friends." David said with an enthusiastic voice.

"Yeah, I already ask her if she wanted to go. I don't know whose clothes she's going to wear." Kaisen answered.

"Harriett probably has an extra pair she can barrow." Harper commented. "I'll text her and ask." He pulled a cell phone from his pocket as he filled his plate with food.

"Why do I need someone else's clothes?" I asked Marilyn.

"Grufon dunes are sand dunes; you will need special clothing for protection from the coarse sand; it also helps keep the sand from getting everywhere." She explained to me then turned toward Kaisen. "You boys better be safe, and be back before dinner, I want to have at least some time with you before you have to go back to school."

"Harriett said she has something you can wear," he said, "so, lets' go." He stood up as he stuffed the last bit of food into his mouth.

"Grab your clothes, Harper and get in my car, I have to get my stuff." Kaisen gestured us towards the garage as he went for the staircase.

When Kaisen got into the driver's side door of his black Camaro, Harper exclaimed, "What is that smell?" It only took me half a second to get a whiff of the strong smell of men's cologne. "Smells like you swam in a bath tub of Potpourri. What are you trying to do, suffocate us? I think I would prefer the smell of B.O. other than that strong crap."

"Shut it!" Kaisen said. I could see his eyes shift in the rear view mirror. It looked like he was looking at me, but he could have been looking out the window. The rest of the ride was quite. I sat back and listened to the radio, not bothering to try to look out the windows. The bucket seats made it hard to see out. Eventually, we pulled up to a huge house a little bigger than David's house.

"What are we doing here?" I asked.

"This is Connor and Jessie Darby's house. They are taking us over to the dunes." Kaisen explained.

We got out of the car and headed towards the house, just then, two girls and three boys came out of the front door and walked towards us. They were all wearing similar clothing, motocross outfits like Harper. When I glanced over to Kaisen I noticed he was wearing the same. All the outfits looked different except Kaisen and another boy looked exactly the same. They were both in red with yellow accents. The two girls looked like professionals in their outfits. One girl wore baby blue, the other in orange. The girl in baby blue carried a pink and black bundle under her arm and a black pair of boots.

"Hey guys, this is Charlotte." Harper introduced me. "This is Harriett, Jessie, Connor, Bubba and Dean. Don't worry about memorizing names, though, they answer to anything." Harper joked with me. "Are those the clothes for her?" He motioned towards the bundle under Harriett's arm.

"Yeah, come with me, you can change in the house before we go. You guys can go get the chopper ready. We will be right back." Harriett said as she and Jessie headed me into the house.

The clothes fit, and the girls were very nice, I wondered how old they were and if I would be going to school with them.

"It fits perfect." Harper said as the other boys looked up at me as we walked into a large machine shed behind the house. It took me a second to realize he meant my outfit.

I was barely paying attention anymore when I noticed the huge helicopter sitting in the middle of the shed. "What is that for?" I asked, stunned.

Kaisen said, "This is what we are riding in up to the dunes, we can't drive to where we are going."

"Well, we could but I don't think you want to ride in a dune buggy for two hours." A boy in silver added. I think his name is Connor.

We finally got up into the air, we only flew for about twenty minutes when Kaisen, Dean, Bubba, and Harriett stood up and grab their snowboards and helmets. They started to strap their snowboards to their boots and went over to the door of the chopper.

"What are they doing?" I asked Jessie, who was sitting next to me.

"Just watch, it's really cool." She smiled at me.

Just as we started to get closer to the ground, I realized what they were about to do. We were probably eight feet in the air when Bubba threw open the door, and before I could stop him, Bubba jumped from the moving helicopter.

"Oh my… I can't believe he just did that." I exclaimed in horror.

Next, Dean jumped then Harriett, and finally I watched as Kaisen leaped into the air and landed on the sandy waves. My heart tried to jump out of my chest as I watched them all. They got smaller and smaller as I noticed we were flying away, leaving them alone in the desert.

"Where are we going?"

"We are going to get the buggies. Can you drive?" Jessie asked.

"I have never driven one before but I could try." I said, half breathing and half gasping.

We got to the buggies and a small shack in the middle of nowhere ten minutes later.

"Just follow me," Harper said right before he took off in one of the buggies. I followed as best I could, through the sand and over the steep dunes. I had to go fast, which I wasn't very good at, but we eventually reach the others. They were sitting on the bottom of one of the dunes, when we got there.

"What took so long?" Bubba asked us. No one answered.

"Ready to race?" Dean asked as the boys smiled. "I'll take the green buggy with Bubba. Kaisen and Harper can go in the blue one, Jessie and Harriett can take the yellow and Connor can take Charlotte in the Orange."

"Hey, wait a minute, that's not fair you always take Bubba and the green buggy. I'll take Bubba and the green buggy and you can take Jessie." Harriett complained.

"Okay, fine." Dean started. "You can take the green one, but I want blue and I want to go with Harper."

Kaisen stepped in to break up the quarrel quickly. "Stop! Dean and Harper in the blue, Bubba and Harriett in the green, the twins in yellow and I'll take Charlotte in the orange. Same course as normal, you know the rules, and it doesn't matter what color you get because I'm going to win."

"As long as you don't cheat," Dean said, "You're going to eat the sand from my tires."

Somehow everyone agreed to that arrangement and I felt scared but satisfied that I got to ride with Kaisen. He seemed like the safest driver out of all of them.

"Why does it matter what color buggy everyone gets?" I asked Kaisen as we started towards our orange buggy.

"Everyone thinks the green one is fastest, because the person who wins usually drives the green one." Kaisen started. "I usually drive the green one, and I usually win." His smile was intoxicating. I smiled back at him before jumping into the passenger seat and strapping myself in.

We started the race in the back next to Bubba and Harriet in the green buggy, but we weren't in the back for long. Kaisen drove like a pro racer, drifting in and out of the other buggies and got out in front and lead the rest up and over the piles of sand through the invisible race track. The wind flew in my face as we went around sharp turns. A couple of times, I could have sworn the buggy was riding on two wheels. The ride was fast and exhilarating even though I was deathly afraid of going fast and was paranoid of getting into a wreck. I tried not to worry about the steep vertical drops and the sharp curves in our path. I loved every minute and I felt safe no matter how dangerously close we were to tipping over. The wind picked up speed as we did and the sand got thicker in the air. I could tell we were nearing the finish because we picked up speed, I couldn't see behind me but I assumed the other buggies were right behind us. I could see a long stretch of flat ground as we barreled over a hill. We came off the hill with a lot of speed and curved around the last mound of sand drifting on what seemed again to be two wheels. I held on tight to the bars on each side of my seat. Kaisen whipped the buggy towards the straight away. I eased myself towards Kaisen a little bit trying to read the speedometer. If I could see correctly, we were going 85 miles-per-hour. We past the only tree I noticed in the whole race and slowed quickly. I knew then we had won the race. Shortly after we slowed and came to a stop I saw the blue buggy follow behind us.

"Jeeze, Kaisen, you're a lead foot." Dean complained. "You could at least have let us believe we were catching up to you."

The yellow buggy flew up barely slowing and stopped. Jessie pulled off her helmet and goggles in one swift movement and motioned for us. "Harriet and Bubba flipped in the last curve." Jessie said in an unconcerned voice.

Dean and Kaisen jumped on the back of the yellow buggy right away and they rode off towards the green buggy.

"Hey, get in." Harper called to me. We got into the blue buggy and followed the others. When we got there Kaisen, Dean, and Connor were lifting the buggy back onto its wheels. It looked like they rolled once and landed on Bubba's side. I was terrified someone was hurt, but no one else seemed concerned. When the wheels were back on the ground Bubba and Harriett both climbed out of the buggy.

"Maybe I should stick to the green buggy. I at least can get out of it if I tip." Kaisen joked.

"We wouldn't have tipped but tubby over here thinks it's alright to whip the sucker full speed around the outside of the normal path." Harriett complained about Bubba's driving. Bubba was a pretty big guy. He was like a huge teddy bear and looked like he couldn't hurt a fly. He reminded me of one of those large Hawaiian guys you see in the movies. He had the dark complexion and black spiky hair that matched perfect.

"Oh, Harriett you're just mad we came in last." Bubba said back. He ignored her after that; he turned to the rest of us. "I'm hungry, let's eat?" Everyone laughed.

"We just got here." Harper said.

"Round two?" Connor asked.

"Green!" Jessie exclaimed.

"Kaisen!" Harriett cried.

"Orange" Dean said.

"It's not the buggy that wins, it's the driver." Kaisen said. "You guys can give me any color buggy and any partner but I'll still win."

"Okay then, you can have Bubba and the orange kart, I'll take Charlotte and the green, and everyone else can keep same riders." Harriett challenged.

"No problem." Kaisen agreed.

This time, I didn't feel as safe. I wasn't sure if it was because I didn't know Harriett or because she was tinier then me and didn't seem like she would be able to keep the large kart upright. I held on tight and let the wind and sand whip along my clothes. I think I was getting sand in the collar of my gear. I watched as the blue kart sped past and then orange flew past at almost twice the speed, then it passed the blue buggy and kept going. The farther we raced the faster we got and the sharper the turns became. Then, without any warning, our buggy was jolted forward by a powerful force from behind. The kart started sliding sideways, throwing lots of sand against my goggles, making it impossible to see. I was terrified at first but then Harriett grabbed my wrist, which made me feel very calm and secure, with one hand and a handle on the roll cage with the other. She hollered what sounded like hold on tight. I was already holding on as tight as I could when the buggy rolled onto Harriett's side then kept going, rolling all the way over and still rolling. My instinct was to close my eyes, but I just sat there and watched as my head started to spin. We finally came to a stop after doing three complete barrels; the kart landed back on its wheels, and I gasped for air, not realizing I had been holding my breath.

"Are you alright?" Harriett asked looking over to me as she shook my wrist she was still holding on to.

"Yeah, are you?"

"Yep, that was fun," She added with a laugh. At first I thought she was crazy but I thought about what just happened and it was fun, it didn't hurt at all. I smiled back at her as she released my hand and pushed on the gas. We lost the race, but rolling was much more exciting. We switched teams up and raced a few more times.

"Don't tell Marilyn you rolled in the buggy, she will be mad we weren't more careful with you the first time we took you somewhere." Kaisen said with a breath taking smile.

"I won't tell. And thanks for inviting me; I had a lot of fun." I smiled back at him.

After getting the buggies rounded up and put back where they belong, the helicopter flew us back to the Darby's house, where we ate turkey sandwiches and talked about our trip to Grufon Dunes. I finally felt like I fit in. Everyone was nice to me, I was even invited to come back and hang out any time I wanted to, and I couldn't wait to see what other things they did for fun here. Even though we only played at Grufon Dunes for an hour and a half, I was wiped out. I slept in the car on the way back to David's house.

"Hey guys, did you have fun?" Marilyn greeted us as we walked into the front door.

"Yeah, I came in second to Kaisen every time but other than that it was great." Harper told her.

"Kaisen you should let someone else win for a change. Just because you can win doesn't always mean you should." Marilyn told him.

"That makes no sense." Kaisen grinned.

"Just give someone else a chance next time, alright. You win too much." Marilyn asked in a sharp but polite way.

"Yes, mother." Kaisen tried to look gloomy.

I really just wanted to curl up with a good book and lay in bed. So that's what I did. I went to the library. I looked for a book with an uninteresting cover, then read the back or inside cover of the book to see what it was about. I did this for several minutes until I came across a small bright green book. It looked old and it was the date on the inside said 1945. I read the first page and it seemed interesting enough to keep my attention for a couple hours until dinner time. I walked back to my room, just before I got to my door, Kaisen and Harper rounded the corner and started walking towards me, to their rooms, I assumed. Harper was still in his motocross outfit but Kaisen was wearing something similar to me, a pair of sweat pants and a t-shirt.

"Gonna take a nap before dinner?" Harper asked me, as he eyed my outfit.

"No, just going to read for a little while." I said as I held my book up for them to see it.

"Oh, okay, we'll see you later then." Harper said.

"Yep… oh and thanks for taking me with you guys today. I had a lot of fun." I added.

"Good. You can come with us any time." Harper beamed.

"Thanks." I said as I glanced at Kaisen's face just before I disappeared into my room. I don't remember falling asleep, but when I opened my eyes my book was lying open on my chest and my clock read six twenty four. Someone would be up to get me soon; dinner always starts at six thirty.

The week went by fast, too fast. Harper, Kaisen and I hung out every day this week. We played board games, video games and watched movies. They even had Jessie and Connor Darby over for a camp fire one evening. Kaisen was getting ready to go back to college and we only had two weeks left until school started. This whole summer went by too quickly.

Chapter 6

Dear Charlotte,

Louis and I miss you, too. Louis will be starting kindergarten and is real excited. I found a house on the other side of the city over by Louis' school; we will be moving there in two weeks. It has three bedrooms, so there is plenty of room whenever you want to visit. Good Luck in school. We love you.

Luke and Louis

FRIDAY NIGHT I was doing my usual routine in the library when I hear the door from behind me open very slowly. It was Harper wearing an unusual outfit. He looked like he came out of a super hero movie. He was wearing what looked like a heavy plastic vest of armor with a black circle in the center.

"What are you doing?" Harper said as he leaned over my computer chair.

"Checking my email." I replied. Harper was pretty cool; he was fun to be around, too.

"What are you doing after that?" Harper said.

"I don't know, probably read until dinner."

"Oh, well, I'm having some friends over and we are going to play laser tag. It might sound childish but it's really fun." He said almost in a shy tone.

"Okay," I said.

I finally figured out what the mystery virtual reality room next to the boys' room was. It was for laser tag. I watched as Harper set everything up. He turned the large screen on and tapped the button that read "alien planet." I watched as the room transformed from a dull black to a deep red. Rock structures protruded from the vertical slits in the walls. The ceiling turned to night and the lights dimmed. I waited for Harper's friends to arrive then they explained the rules. They placed a heavy vest on me and fastened it in place.

"All you have to do is shoot everyone except me; I'm on your team. Don't get shot. The more you shoot the less ammo your gun will have so lift it up so it points at the ceiling and pull the reload button back. Got it?" Harper explained.

"I think so." I replied, examining my gun and heavy vest that I was wearing.

Once I was ready, the game started. Harper and I ducked down behind rocks and we stayed together for the most part. Harper was really good at this game. I watched as he shot everyone he saw, and he never missed. I heard a creaking noise behind me. I turned around and pulled the trigger for the first time. Harriet had snuck up on me. She shot me and my vest lit up and I had to wait fifteen seconds before I could shoot my gun. I kept close to Harper, making sure no one shot him.

Finally I was getting the hang of it. I walked backwards as Harper walked forward, he shot the people in front, I shot everyone in back of us. By the end of the game I had thirteen kills and died twenty three times. I did pretty well for my first time, but not compared to everyone else. Harper managed to get thirty one kills and only died eight times. We played the first game for thirty minutes. The next game we played was forty-five minutes. I was having so much fun, I didn't even realize I hadn't eaten in hours and I was hungry.

"Thanks for asking me to play laser tag with you guys, it was a lot of fun." I told Harper as we walked together down for dinner.

"No problem, you can hang out with me and my friends anytime you want. Actually tomorrow we might go fishing, you are welcome to come." He said kindly.

I LIED IN BED for a few seconds, trying to wake up all the way. Once I ate my breakfast, showered and was completely up for the day, I went to the library for a new book. The last one I read was about some man lost in the woods and lived there for years. I wasn't into books like that. The library was my favorite place in the house. I walked around the large room in and out of the isles of books. There was one isle I never went in, because it was so far in the back that I never made it that far without finding a good book. I decided to start there first. There were a lot of thick books in the back of the library. One tattered brown book caught my eye. I pulled it off the book case and looked it over. The binding was made from animal hide and it must have weighed fifteen pounds. The pages were made of thick parchment and the ink on the pages were hand written, not typed. It didn't look like an actual story book, but it's old and interesting. I carefully opened the front cover. The book didn't have a title, but there was a message scratched into the first page that read…

> To my beloved Geo Bain, you are my one and only.
> Celia Bain

I flipped to the next page and read The Cigam-Bain Family History printed in a swirly calligraphy. The next two pages made a family tree with names of the Cigam-Bain family and the Date of Birth and Death under each name. As I read through the people, I came across Geo-Bain and Celia, they were married for 75 years but both passed away on the same day. Under their name were their children, Marilyn and Vivianne. Next to Marilyn's name was a dark black mark where a name used to be, and below those two names was Kaisen and Harper. Once I noticed that this book was Kaisen and Harper's family history, I was intrigued. I kept reading, family history is always interesting, even if it's not my own.

I thumbed through some of the entries that family members left inside, only stopping to read a few things, then went through the rest of the book. There were a few pictures of animals that I have never seen and most of the book is in a different language, there is an index that translates some of it, but I don't understand what it means even when it's in English. Most of the pages talked about a city named Andeka, which I assumed to be the family's hometown. As I put the book back onto the shelf, I see another old book, but this one is much smaller. It resembles a journal; I pull it off the shelf and feel the crushed leather binding. There is a strange design on the front cover that I have seen before. I don't remember where, it just seems familiar. I open up to the first page of the journal and see that the title is typed, not hand written. It reads 'Andeka: Histories and Prophecies.' Just in curiosity I turn the page. It's in English. I read the first few sentences and became so confused that I pulled out the Cigam-Bain family History book again, and then I re-read the first paragraph of the history and prophecies journal.

Andeka is a vast world hidden in the forests of Europe for years when humans banished The Cigam from the non-magical world. A treaty between the Cigam and Humans was passed in the year 312 stating that the Cigam could no longer live among the humans and humans could not live among the Cigam. To avoid war and constant fighting between worlds, the Cigam closed the portal linking the two similar species. Only the Supreme Rulers and Politicians of the worlds have the abilities to pass into and out of the worlds.

I didn't stop at the first paragraph; I kept reading and found myself lost between the pages of the journal, not worrying if I'm reading fact or fiction, just captivated by the story.

Two-hundred years after the treaty was signed, changes started happening for Andeka. A young Cigam named Guin-Bock was discovered to be the number one most powerful Cigam in all of Andeka. He possessed a new power that no other Cigam has ever had. Guin-Bock took power of Andeka as supreme ruler. He brought Andeka out of the depths of poverty and created a new system of power. He ruled for 12 years alone when he found and married Pia Val-Che, a wealthy Cigam. Each losing their spouses years before, they bring their families together.

After years of ruling, Guin-Bock and Pia decided to divide Andeka into four regions, giving each of their four sons part of the Andeka throne. Pia's two sons: Che and Bain, and Guin-Bock's two sons: Flink and Cigam, now each had their own piece of Andeka, while Guin-Bock stayed supreme ruler, he watched over them, kept them from fighting each other and kept Andeka safe. Guin-Bock and Pia stay in Youffe Castle in Brevil the first Capital Castle at the heart of Andeka...

I recognize some of the places and names in the 'history' section of the journal. I open the Cigam-Bain Family history book back up and look through the family tree again. At the very top of the tree is the name Pia Val-Che. She has a birth date but no death date. Then I skim down her line her two sons were (obviously) also on the tree. I only have to go down about fifteen generations when I reach Marilyn. Many of the people have date of death, but they all lived unbelievably long. Most of the dates state that the people lived to be over four hundred years old. That really can't be possible, can it? I don't know why, but I have a strong feeling in my chest that it's true, that everything that I have just read, no matter how ridiculous it sounds, I know that it’s real. After an overwhelming feeling wash over me, I keep reading, needing to know more. I flip through the pages of the family history book once more. I come to a page that is titled 'The Powers of the Cigam.'

Each Cigam has his or her own power/gifts. Each one is unique to the Cigam and strengthens with practice and confidence. The most common gifts are those of the two sons of Val-Che: Cigam-Che and Cigam-Bain. They can be the easiest to learn but hardest to fully master. A Cigam-Che has the ability to hover over the earth. The gift starts out powerful, in the beginning of a Cigam's training with their gifts, they find it very hard to control them, but after about a week of training, it starts to get easier. A Cigam isn't required to learn their gifts until they have completed the first thirteen years of normal human schooling. Once they have completed the thirteenth year, they go on to a special school for controlling and strengthening their gifts. While they are learning to control their gifts they choose a career that suits their gifts and they train to get the most use out of their powers during their jobs. This schooling can take anywhere from three to eight years. Flinks and rare gifted Cigam take much longer than the more common gifts and careers.

I kept skimming through some of the information, only reading bits and pieces. Then I came across a list of the different Cigam.

Che- the ability to hover over the earth; if mastered the cigam will have the ability to fly

Bain- the ability to travel through the air by transportation. As the power is strengthened, the cigam can take items with them, such as people or vehicles.

Flink- A Flink is a Cigam with two gifts instead of just one. Example: Che-Bain can hover and transport.

Hue- the ability to manipulate the mind and feelings

Shaire- the ability to use other Cigams gifts when they are in a close proximity, if mastered they can use the gifts of other Cigam when they are no longer around

Loss- the ability to persuade someone's mind into thinking a certain way (not as strong as Hue)

Brink- the ability to bring luck into a Cigam's life

Vou- the ability to persuade into agreement (not as strong as Loss)

Sweud- the rare ability to disappear

Dau- the ability to keep healthy and can live longer than the usual Cigam. A Dau can use their powers to keep others healthy and to heal small wounds.

Waek- the ability to calm people

Segoe- the ability to heal any wound

Jube- the rare ability to see future events before they happen. When mastered they can see things as far as thousands of years in the future.

Yeno- the ability of speed

Ameir- the ability to make someone fall in love

Trog- the ability of strength

Yake- the ability to hide one's self from certain things, doesn't disappear, just blends in or changes the imagination to think they look different than they actually look.

Orve-the ability to shield themselves from other Cigam's gifts

Quaro- the ability to predict what will happen or to see the gifts of other Cigam

Shaire-Hue- the ability to manipulate anything that is made from energy with his mind and can use any other power and has the ability to harness the power of all the Dekian

Crystals. Guin-Bock is the only Shaire-Hue in existence so far. (Continues in Andeka's Prophecy.)

I quickly stopped reading the list and turned to Andeka's Prophecy, to find out more. I read through the different prophecies over the years until I came across the prophecy about Guin-Bock.

Guin-Bock and Pia Val-Che will maintain the status of Supreme Ruler until Guin-Bock's true identical is discovered. A true identical will be the only other Shaire-Hue and will take the place as Supreme Ruler when found. The True identical will be the only Cigam that will be able to regain Andeka to its former glory. The true identical will have the power to pull Andeka out of poverty and end the oncoming wars that will plague Andeka years before the true identical is found. Without the true identical, Andeka will be destroyed by powerful but evil Cigam that fight for the throne of the four kingdoms and the capital city, where the supreme ruler is located. Only the heir to the Andeka thrones has the ability and the courage to search for the true identical. Each heir to the Andeka Kingdoms has their own destiny in the locating of the true identical. Many will not live out their destiny that has been set for them, but the ones who do will be graciously rewarded.

I kept flipping and skimming page after page of information, not knowing what I should think about all of this. I read about the different animals in Andeka and the language. I found a few things about Dekian Crystals, but couldn't find much.

The more I read the more real Andeka and the Cigam became. I thought I would go crazy with all this information.

Powers, a secret world, creatures undiscovered by humans. I wasn't sure if I could believe it. Even though Marilyn and her two sons are inside this strange book, I can't be sure that this isn't just a make believe book from the boys childhood.

I read a few more things and then looked on the book shelf where I found the history book, to look for anything else that could help me figure this out. I was lucky. I actually found two dictionaries full of Dekia and another large book that looked just like the Cigam-Bain Family History book. I snuck them back to my room. I was pretty sure if David has kept this a secret from me for this long, they didn't want me to know, so I wasn't going to tell David or Marilyn yet. Maybe I can talk to Harper about this.

I memorized a few sentences that I would try out on Harper later. The dictionaries said that the Cigam language was ancient and not many practiced the language anymore, but maybe Harper will know since it says he is a descendant from Pia Val-Che. I put away the dictionaries and picked up a different book that I took from the library. This book was made out of the same animal hide and thick parchment as the Cigam-Bain Family History book. I opened the book and read *The Cigam-Flink Family History*. I turned the page and found that this book and the Cigam-Bain book are the same, just for different families. Everything in both books is organized the same. The page I flipped to was the family tree. This time it starts with Guin-Bock, instead of Pia Val-Che, so this was the other half of the royal family. I looked through the tree and as I got down to the bottom, a name caught me by surprise and I dropped the book. I took a deep breath, gathered my thoughts and picked up the book, opened it back up to the family tree and took a closer look at my name that was scratch below my father's.

Knock, Knock, Knock.

I threw the books under my pillow and sprinted to the door before someone could open it. I cracked the door a little bit and peeked my head out.

“Yes?” I asked trying not to look suspicious.

“Lunch is ready.” Harper said. I had been reading about Andeka for nearly four hours. Harper gave me a weird glance. “What are you up to?” He smirked.

“Nothing,” I smiled. I needed to think of a lie to tell him before he really tried to get me to tell him, I wasn't sure what power he had and I didn't want to know if it was a sort of mind control. “I was talking with my friend Holly, from back home. We were gossiping that's all.” I smiled again, passing by him and shutting my door behind me as I started to walk down the hall towards the stairs.

When I got back up to my room I pulled out the history about my own family. I should have guessed that I could be a part of this, but it didn't register until I saw that I was a direct descendant of Guin-Bock, the ruler of Andeka. I was overwhelmed by all of this information, but I had to know more. The rest of the day I read about Andeka, the Cigam and tried to figure out what else was going on.

THE NEXT MORNING I woke up early. I couldn’t decide if the sun woke me or if it was the banging noise coming from outside my window. I walked onto the balcony out my bedroom window to see what was going on. A man with a tool belt, whom I had never met before was hammering nails into some kind of wooden structure. I watched curiously until I saw David waving up at me. He was talking with another man who was also wearing a tool belt. David motioned for me to come join him down stairs. I quickly changed into a pair of day clothes and hurried down to see him. I couldn't stop thinking about Andeka but I knew that I shouldn't ask about it, not until I know more about it just in case David takes the books away.

"What's going on?" I asked David.

"Marilyn and I are having a wine tasting and end of summer party tonight. Did we wake you?"

"Yes, but that's alright. I'm hungry I think I'm going to have some breakfast."

"I will join you." David said as he walked with me into the house.

Later on in the early afternoon, Connor and Jessie came over to go fishing with Harper and me. I don't go fishing often but I thought it would be a fun experience and it would give me a chance to pay attention and see if any of them talk about Andeka, besides I wouldn't get much reading done while the workers hammered away outside my window.

"So, Harper have you heard about Bala lately?" Jessie asked.

"Uh," Harper started as he looked over at me, then back to Jessie. "No… I can't believe school is starting Monday. This summer went by so fast." I wasn't sure if Harper had changed the subject or if that was what Jess was talking about.

We walked through the grassy meadow behind the large hedge maze until we reached the lake. I could see it from my bedroom window but had never been this far before. The lake had a wooden dock on the closest edge to where we were standing. I could see a small building on the opposite side of the lake and another dock. The lake had to have been almost a half a mile long and a quarter of a mile wide. The water was a pretty blue from far away but once we got up close, it was hard to see through the water at all.

The four of us sat at the edge of the dock and since I hadn't been fishing in a while, Harper baited my hook for me. We all cast out into the water and waited. We were all dead silent for almost ten minutes before Connor's line started to pull. He pulled his pole upwards as he tried to stand up.

"I think I've got one." Connor exclaimed. We all watched as Connor wrestled with the fish on the other end. It only took a few moments for the fish to float up to the top of the water and for Harper to catch it with the net. It was a small sunfish not even five inches long. Connor pulled the hook from its mouth and released it back into the water. After waiting a few more moments my line started to pull a bit. I started cranking the reel slowly, not to let the fish escape. When I got the fish to the top of the water, like Connor did, Harper placed the net in the water and scooped up my fish. It was even smaller then Connor's had been. Harper took the fish of the hook for me and placed it back in the water. After a few more catches, Jessie finally caught one big enough to keep. It was a Catfish. Jessie put on a rubber glove to hold on to the fish while she used pliers to remove the hook. It was probably twelve inches long. Connor helped Jessie put the fish on a stringer so they could place it into the water without it getting away.

"That's a nice fish Jess," Harper complimented as he cast his line back out into the water. Jess smiled back at him without saying anything. It wasn't long after when Harper's line started to pull. He stood up to get better balance and his foot slipped off the edge of the dock. He fell forward into the water, still holding onto his fishing pole. He made a splash that soaked most of his spot and some of Connor's. We all started to laugh, until Harper's head came up from under the water. We tried to stop laughing right away but it didn't work well.

"Want some help?" Connor asked as he knelt down on the edge and offered his hand to Harper. Harper looked at his hand and reached for it. Then he grinned as he pulled Connor towards the water. Jessie and I were standing behind Connor when Connor reached up and grabbed Jessie's hand and they both went into the water.

"Your turn, Charlotte." Harper called to me.

"I don't think so." I said smiling. Harper came to the side of the dock and tried grabbing my leg. I jumped back before he could reach me. I watched as Harper swam to the ladder attached to the dock. I started walking up towards the meadow before Harper could get out.

"Charlotte, come back." Harper called to me. I didn't hear him come up behind me, but I felt a wet hand around my waist. I tried to pull away but Harper is much stronger then I am. He pulled me towards him and threw me over his shoulder like I was a sack of potatoes. We started laughing as he ran me back to the side of the dock. I was almost too distracted to realize that there was only one set of foot prints on the dock. There should be two. I did a double take as I saw that the one set of foot marks were Harper's as he carried me back from the meadow. I didn't make any because my feet are dry but there should be two sets of Harper's; ones coming and one going. I wanted to point it out right then but Jessie and Connor were around and I wasn't sure if they knew or were even allowed to know.

"Ready? Hold your breath." Harper said right before he jumped and we both plunged into the lake.

We played in the water for a while, forgetting about the fish. We brought the one fish back that Jessie caught. We all watched as Chef Mallow cleaned and cooked the fish. Later that night I went back through the list of Cigam powers. If Andeka is a real place and Cigam exist and Harper is one, which would explain how he got to me so fast and how he didn't leave any foot prints on the dock earlier.

It sunk in a little more that this could actually be real. I had a feeling it was real and since no one knows what I know, I don't have to feel stupid about this if it turns out to be fake. Anyways, if Harper is a Cigam and he does have gifts then he could be a Bain or a Che. Che was sort of like transporting from one place to another. Bain is more like hovering or flying. I don't know how he did either of these things without Jessie and Connor seeing, but for all I know they are Cigam too. What really had me intrigued was the fact that my name was on the tree under Guin-Bock, which means that I am a Cigam. That means that I might have a power. That really blew my mind. The second I thought about the possibilities, I felt a warm sensation cross my body, from then on I felt different. I read through the beginning again, 'The Cigam's power can't manifest without the belief that they are actually there.' I knew after that I really was a Cigam, Harper was too, and I am part of something bigger than I ever imagined. I want to know more, I want to know what a Cigam actually entails, and I want to know what powers I possess. The book says that Cigam's usually had similar powers to the parents, but I don't know what David's power is so I can't figure out mine. All I can do is keep reading and learning about the history of Andeka and eventually talk to someone about it.

AS I DRESSED FOR SCHOOL I wondered what the schools here would be like. I wondered if I would have any classes with Harper or any of my other new friends. I had to admit, I was pretty nervous. I did well at my old school but I wasn't sure if this would be the same. After breakfast, Harper drove us to the high school. It seemed to be in the middle of nowhere. There were no other buildings or houses surrounding the school that I could tell. The parking lot was on the right side of the building. Harper walked me to the main office where we both picked up our schedules and to my relief we had the first two classes together. He promised to show me around before our first class started.

The school was huge. The main office was the first building from the parking lot. There were six other buildings. Each was assigned for specific subjects. The Gym and Sports Center was next to the main office. Then the sidewalk leads to each different building: Math, Sciences, English, Social Studies, and Arts. I like that the school was broken up by subject, it would be much easier to find my classes. I wasn't too excited about having to walk to class in the cold during the winter but I would have to get over that.

I sat next to Harper in our first class, Early Civilization. In our second class, Chemistry, the teacher had us placed into assigned seats paired in groups of two at lab tables. I was paired with Jessie Darby. I was relieved I was with someone I already knew. It probably would have been easy to make new friends but having someone I know as a lab partner was better, I already knew I could trust her and she was able to come over and help with homework, if we needed. I compared class schedules with Jessie during the beginning of the teachers lecture. We had lunch together, then Calculus after that. She said Connor had writing strategies with me right after this class, which was a relief. I walked with him, but was on my own for Poetry and Short Stories class, but I managed to find it just fine.

I only had seven classes because I was a senior and didn't need the last credit so I chose not to take an extra class. Harper only had seven classes as well so after my economics class I met him in the parking lot by his car.

"How was your first day?" He asked on our way home.

"It was like any other first day, I guess. All of my teachers seem nice and I know someone in almost all my classes." I told him.

"That's good. This year better go by fast, my classes are going to be a breeze. Oh, that reminds me, Dean is throwing a start of the school year party, do you want to come?"

"Tonight?" I asked.

"No, it's going to be Friday night." He said, trying to hold back a laugh.

"Oh, that makes sense. Yeah, sounds fun."

FRIDAY CAME FASTER THAN I expected. My first week of class had passed without a skip of a beat. I had all my homework done by five o'clock every night. The teachers gave lots of reading assignments, which I didn't particularly like, so I got those done first. My Calculus teacher gave us a syllabus with a schedule of all the homework assignments due for the entire semester; so of course, I had the whole weeks' worth of math done before Wednesday. I also had Monday and Tuesday's homework done, I didn't want to get too far ahead.

"HARPER, I WANT you both back by 12:00 tonight." Marilyn told us while we were eating dinner Friday night."

"But mom, that is no time at all." Harper complained.

"Well I don't want you two out too late, you know what happened last year. I don't want to have to stay up late worrying."

"Mom, nothing is going to happen. We will be fine, we know the rules and we aren't going to do anything stupid, I promise." Harper said. "Can we please stay out until one?"

"12:30, but that is the latest. Don't push it Harper, or you won't go at all." Marilyn said as a vein popped out of her forehead. I have never seen her so worried. She is very intimidating when she wants to be.

"Fine, we'll be back at 12:30. Can we go, now?" He asks as he pushes himself back from the table.

"Drive safe and be careful." Marilyn says sternly as Harper and I get up from the table.

"We will, mom." He said.

"WHAT HAPPENED LAST year at this party? Your mom said that you know what happened last year." I asked when we got into the car.

"Mom always makes a big deal out of this every time I go to a party. I was seeing this girl and she went to the party last year with me. The other girls started a truth or dare game and to make a long story short. Everyone ended up skinny dipping in the lake and the girl that I was supposed to be there with hooked up with her old boyfriend while we were there and got pregnant."

"Oh my gosh, that's terrible."

"The terrible thing is she didn't tell me that she hooked up with him so we kept dating like nothing happened. So when she started to show everyone thought it was mine, including my mom. She didn't believe me when I told her it wasn't mine. I was grounded for a month. I broke it off with that girl and asked her to talk to my mom and tell her that we never did anything together. Which is true, I never had sex with her. I was so mad, I really liked her, but I didn't want to be with her after she lied to me and cheated."

"I am so sorry, Harper." I said, shocked.

"Don't be, everything worked out for the best. She is engaged to her baby's dad and she finished school early.

"Do you still talk to...?" I started, as I glanced at Harper I saw something out of the corner of my eye, once I turned to look it was too late. “Harper!” I screamed, sucking in a gasp as he turned his attention back to the road just in time to see the large animal darting across the road in front of the car. I threw my arms up to cover my face and when I did, for a split second everything around me stopped. I wasn't sure how but everything around me was frozen, like I pressed pause on a remote somewhere. As soon as I realized what was happening I released my grasp and everything resumed. I felt a jolt as Harper stomped onto the brake, but the animal was too close. Everything happened so fast. I closed my eyes as I anticipated the impact. I heard sound of shattering of glass around me and then the whole car shook. The back end fish tailed, whirling the vehicle around like a ride at an amusement park. The car shook again, I knew what was going to happen next, I felt déjà vu coming. I remember this feeling from when I was in the dune buggy a few weeks ago. This time I didn’t think I was going to have as much fun as I did then. The car rolled onto its side and kept going until it landed upside down. When I opened my eyes I could see a dark brown heap of fur a few yards away in the middle of the road. I was so shaken; I didn’t know what to do. I couldn’t feel any pain at all; I assumed that was from the adrenaline pumping through me. I was upside down and my seat belt had braced me from falling. I looked over to see if Harper was alright. I couldn’t see him well, the airbag on his side had deployed.

“Harper?” I tried to say, that’s when I noticed my throat hurt, it was scratchy and I felt like my throat was full of glass. I started to panic and I started to cough, which just hurt worse. “Harper?” I said, as a lump rose in my throat but no tears came to my eyes. I suddenly felt helpless and alone. I wasn't sure what to do.

Get out of the car. That's all my mind was saying. Get out of the car. The windshield and back window were both shattered and my window was gone. I reached over and turned the car off, but kept the lights on. That's when I saw the blood on my hand and I started to panic again. Where was that coming from? I still didn't feel any pain, other than my throat. I patted myself down real good to find any damage, nothing. Maybe the blood was from Harper. I hoped I was wrong. I braced myself while I took my seat-belt off. My arms gave way when the seat-belt no longer held up my body; I was a lot heavier than I thought. I tried to crawl from the wreckage very carefully not to cut myself on any of the glass outside my window. It was inevitable though; army crawling on glass and rocks was going to do, at least, some damage. I stood up and stared in horror at the car. How was I supposed to get Harper out of this, should I call the ambulance first? I walked over to Harper's side of the car; there was blood on his window and on the broken windshield. I ran back to my side of the car and searched for my purse. I couldn't reach it from where I was. It was lying on the roof spilled out all over, which was convenient because I could see my phone, and it was right behind Harper's head. I didn't want to go back into the car to get it, but I knew I would need it. I tried to open up my door but it wouldn't budge; the top of the car had been crushed down enough that the door was clamped shut, which made me think again: how am I going to get Harper out of the vehicle? I crawled back into the car, just far enough to reach my phone, then I saw a piece of clothing in the back, it was a jacket, I grabbed that too. I was so flustered I forgot where exactly I was, did Europe use 9-1-1 for emergencies or was that just America? I didn't ponder that question long; I dialed Dad's number, instead.

"Hello?" he answered on the second ring.

"Dad," I panicked, tears started streaming down my face, I was hysterical, my throat hurt as I tried to tell him what had happened. "We hit an animal and Harper is hurt and he won't talk to me and I don't know what to do. I don't know where I am…"

"Charlotte, calm down, it's going to be alright. What happened, I can barely understand you." I could hear the fear in his voice as he was trying to stay under control.

I took a deep breath and started over, this time with more success. "Harper hit an animal with the car, I am fine, but he is still inside the car, it's upside down and he isn't moving."

"Is he breathing?"

"I don't know." More tears rolled down my cheeks, not wanting to know the answer, just in case.

"Listen to me, Charlotte. You have to find out for me. Okay?"

"Okay." I blubbered into the phone.

"Can you reach him?"

"I can if I get back into the car."

"Listen to me; do not get back into the car. Go to his side of the car, is the window broken?" He asked.

"No, it's cracked; I think he hit his head against it. Dad, he is bleeding." I sobbed.

"Charlotte," He paused, I could hear him take a deep breath. "I know this is hard, just try to stay as calm as possible, alright? Now, try to open up his door."

"I can't, it's smashed in too much, and I can't open it."

"Alright, do you have a jacket or long sleeves or something that you can put over your arm? I need you to break the window."

"Yes, I have a jacket."

"I need you to wrap it around your arm, and use your elbow to break the window, it's probably going to hurt, but you need to get Harper out of the car in case another car comes and doesn't see it in time." He stopped for a minute; I could hear him talking to someone in the background. I hoped it wasn't Marilyn. She was going to freak out when she hears about this, especially because she is the one that was talking about us being in a car accident.

I did as he told me. I put down the phone. I knelt down beside the window, took a deep breath, closed my eyes and thrust by arm as hard as I could into the window. I heard a loud cracking sound, the window cracked a little bit more. I tried again, hearing another cracking sound. My elbow throbbed so much, but I tried to ignore the pain as I hit the window again. This cracking sound was a little different, it was a different pitch, I knew that I was almost done. I hit the glass again, this time my elbow went farther than before, traveling straight through the window and stopping just shy of Harper's face. I gasped and unwrapped my arm quickly, and picked the phone back up.

"Alright, dad, I did it."

"Check Harper's pulse. And see if he is breathing."

I held my breath as I felt around his throat to find something to tell me if he… His throat was moving, as well as his chest. Thank God. "He's breathing." I all but shouted with relief.

"Thank Goodness. Okay, Charlotte, I am already on my way, I know what direction you guys would have taken, are there any road signs around you at all?"

I glanced around me but found nothing. "No, I am in the middle of nowhere. Well, there aren't any signs but we went around a curve not far back and I think I can see another one down the road a ways, I know that probably won't help but that's all I see. We are surrounded by trees on both sides of the road."

"That's alright honey, don't worry, I'll find you soon, I need to hang up the phone now. Try to get Harper to wake up, he needs to get out of the car, blood is probably rushing to his head since he is still upside down, be careful with him, though."

"Okay, hurry Dad." I said before the line went dead. I looked around again, not sure what I was searching for, but when I turned my head to look back from where we came from, a gust of wind hit my face. I felt a burning sensation on my forehead. I reached up instinctively to feel it, I hadn't noticed that I was sweating, but my forehead was wet. I followed the sweat as it ran down the side of my face, and even though it was dark out, I could see my hand was covered in something dark; blood. I was bleeding; I must have hit my head, too. I couldn't deal with this right now; I ignored my injury and leaned into Harper's window. "Harper!" I said placing my hands on his shoulders. "Harper!" I called again; no answer. I felt a sense of panic wash over me as I thought of the fire that took away my mother. If I didn't do something Harper might be gone forever too, and I couldn't let that happen.

I placed one of my hands on his back, and let his head rest against my shoulder. Then I released him from his seat-belt quickly, using my free hand to try and guide his body gently to the ground. I got most of his top half out of the car quite easily, but he was a pretty big boy. I rested his back against my knees and opened the jacket up so I could place it underneath him, then with all the strength I had left; I pulled his body out of the car, trying to get leverage with my feet up against the car. When I got all but his legs out, I wrapped my arms underneath his armpits and stood up as best I could, and pulled him out the rest of the way. I drug him as far over to the side of the road as possible. I slipped and landed on my butt, with Harper pulled up onto my legs, I left him there, not wanting to move him anymore. I sat on the side of the road, wrapped my arms around Harper and held him up, waiting for my dad to arrive. "Harper, can you hear me?" I asked him. He moved a little bit, but didn't say anything. "Harper, Harper, wake up." I tried wiggling him. He let out a small moan. "It's going to be okay, we are going to get you to a hospital." I could tell my adrenaline rush was starting to drop; I started to notice aches and pains I hadn't noticed before. I looked Harper up and down, searching for any bad injuries. His head was the only thing bleeding bad enough for stitches. His arms and face were cut up from the glass but I couldn't find any other visible damage.

The lights of a vehicle came up behind us and I could see flashing lights after that. It was my Dad, Chef Mallow and an ambulance.

"Charlotte, are you guys alright?" He asked, as he saw the upside down car.

"Harper won't wake up, he groaned a minute ago and he moved a bit but he won't open his eyes or say anything. Is he going to be okay?"

"I don't know sweetie." He said as he helped me get out from underneath Harper. The paramedics hooked Harper up to monitors inside of the ambulance and checked all of his vitals. They checked me over next. I had a few shards of windshield glass in my throat. They wouldn't be able to see how much damage the pieces have done until I got to the emergency room. They cleaned my hands and arms off and had me feel around in my mouth to see if I could pull any of the glass out. There was nothing big enough to grab a hold of, which was a relief. I felt like I was chewing sand, I could hear the grinding of the small pieces of glass between my teeth. I gargled some water to get out any pieces, so I didn't swallow any more. They had me ride in the ambulance to the hospital, where I had x-rays done to check for any major injuries. I had none, just a bump on the head and lots of bruises, but nothing broken. All the glass was taken out of the inside of my throat. There wasn't a lot but even when the doctors were done, it felt like pieces were still there. They said the glass made small scratches in the thin tissue in my throat. It will heal within a few days and I might have a sore throat and discomfort but the glass didn't do any major damage. And even if I had swallowed any big pieces, the windshield glass is easy to break down in my stomach that it won't be life threatening.

Harper had a concussion, two bruised ribs and a bruised cheek bone, but they said he should be fine. He needed thirteen stitches in his forehead, too. I sat in Harper's hospital room until he woke up two hours after arriving at the hospital. Sitting there, I was reliving the accident over and over, asking myself, did I imagine it or did the accident really stop and then start again. I had almost convinced myself that it hadn't happened when Harper woke up.

"I am so sorry, Charlotte, are you alright," was the first thing that came out of his mouth when he opened his eyes and saw me sitting beside his bed.

"I'm fine. How do you feel?" My throat was scratchy but it didn't hurt as much as it sounded.

"I feel terrible, I can't believe that happened. I should have been paying closer attention to the road, but it just came out of know where. Are you sure you're alright?"

"Harper, it's fine, I'm fine, you're fine, and everything is fine… except the animal…and your car." I added.

"Ugh, my car! Is David mad?"

"No. They are pretty worried about you though. This is actually the first time they have left the room. David went to pick up some food and your mom is out in the hall talking to Kaisen on the phone."

"I bet mom is just dying to tell me 'I told you so.'"

"I don't think she will. We were all really worried. You were out for a few hours. I had to pull you out of the car."

"You did, wow, you must be pretty strong." He joked.

“I was terrified; I don’t know how I did it. I think I got more injuries trying to break out your window then I did from the actual crash.” I said showing him the massive bruise on my right elbow. It extended from my elbow all the way to the middle of my forearm.

“Oh, geez. That looks like it really hurts. I am so sorry. I feel terrible. Thank you though… for taking care of me.”

“You would have done the same thing for me. Plus, we are family, why wouldn’t I do that for you? I’m just glad I didn’t have to do CPR.”

“Harper, how are you feeling?” Marilyn asked as she walked into the room. She was holding the phone up to her ear still. “Kaisen, I'm handing the phone to Charlotte, Harper just woke up.” She handed me the phone and sat down next to Harper.

“Hello,” I said as I took the phone call out into the hall. I hadn't talk to Kaisen at all since he left to go back to school and I wasn't sure what I was going to talk to him about, except maybe a half a minute of I'm fine and nothing is broken.

Like I thought, he asked how I was. I told him what happened and explained my few injuries.

“Well, I'm glad you both are all right. I was in the middle of homework when mom called me. She is so over reactive, that she made everything sound so much worse than it actually is.”

“Yeah, it’s not as bad as she thinks. Well do you need to get back to your homework then?” I ask, hoping to get off the phone, I am not used to talking to Kaisen and I'm not sure what to say.

“No, I will finish it later, mom made me worry so much that I can't do anything right now.” He said as I watched Harper and Marilyn from the window. Harper looked over at me and gave me a weird 'help-me' look.

“Well did you want to talk to Harper?”

“Yeah, thank you.” I walked into the room and smiled at Harper.

“Here he is. It was nice talking to you.” I said.

“Yep, glad you’re alright, feel free to call me anytime if you ever want to talk.” He said before I said good bye and handed Harper the phone.

Harper spent the night in the hospital, but came home early the next morning. His ribs were sore but he acted completely back to normal by the time we had school on Monday. Harper’s car was totaled, but there were plenty of cars in the garage to choose from.

THE FIRST SEMESTER went by quickly and I was making more friends than I thought possible. Everyone at this new school was very nice. It was easy making friends when I played on the volley ball team, was in the honor’s program and I took pictures during most of the soccer and rugby games for the yearbook. When I wasn’t doing school work I was hanging out with Harper or talking to Kaisen on the phone. I remember one night I talked to Kaisen for three hours. I wasn’t sure exactly what we were talking about, but it was easy to talk to him. I had grown a strong attachment for both boys. Harper was just like the older brother I never had, even though he was younger than me. He always stuck up for me if I needed it or helped me with homework and always invited me to come with him when he went places. Kaisen on the other hand was so sweet. I started talking to him after the accident and we talked almost every day since. My stomach fluttered every time my phone rang. I really liked him, he was cute, funny, and sentimental and I felt like I could tell him anything. I didn't know what to do. I wasn't sure if he liked me back. I didn't want to assume he did, just because he talked to me on the phone, I used to talk to my friends on the phone for hours all of the time. They were mostly about boys and gossip, though. I guess I would have to wait and see.

I went to the library when I had gotten back from the hospital. I brought the books back to my room. I didn't have much time to look through the Cigam Family Books, but every once and a while I would take them out from under my bed and read them. I didn't waste my time on the Dekia language; it was too hard to figure out. I was able to put a few sentences together that made sense, but was too afraid to try them out on anyone. I needed to know what I was. I wasn't 100 percent sure but I think I stopped time during the accident. I debated it for a while, but decided that it didn't matter if I did because I was too afraid to ask anyone about it. This semester was over before I knew it, and I was glad when it finally ended. I didn't want to admit it, but I really missed Kaisen, I know we talked almost every day, but I wanted to see him in person. I had a picture of us from the day at Grufon Dunes that is a group shot, but I can still see his large brown eyes.

Winter break started in three days, Harper and I had final exams to take and Kaisen would be here on Friday. I missed him so much. I wasn't sure how to act when he got back. I liked him a lot and I didn't know how to hide it from him and everyone else. I know I wouldn't be able to tell anyone but I didn't know how much longer I would be able to keep this secret bottled up.

Chapter 7

I WAS STARTING to get tired halfway through our game of monopoly.

"All that pop is getting to me, I'll be right back." Harper jumped up quickly and dashed out the door. "No cheating," He called down the hall. I laughed at him softly, so did Kaisen. It was my turn and I reached for the dice at the same time Kaisen did. My heart fluttered as our hands touched. I pulled my hand away but he didn't, he grasped the dice in his hand and handed them to me.

"Thanks," I said awkwardly.

Kaisen laughed, "Sure." He said. I rolled the dice, three. I sucked at this game. I was losing, again. I had lost the game of Sorry we played before this. After a few long minutes of awkward silence and after Kaisen took his turn, we looked at each other. He was so beautiful; his warm chocolate eyes made me want to melt. He didn't look away and I couldn't look away. We sat looking at each other for a few seconds then I saw him lean in towards me. I started to lean as well and as our lips were only inches away, he broke eye contact, standing abruptly and walking to the door.

"Uh, um, I'll… be right back." He said almost in a daze as he rushed out of the room. I took a deep breath and gathered my thoughts. What just happened, were we really leaning in to each other? Was that a sign that he feels something too?

"Harper," Kaisen said as he walked down the hall out of ear shot. "Something just happened with Charlotte."

"What do you mean? Did you make a move?" Harper asked laughing.

"No. She used my power."

"What? How did she do that?" Harper stopped laughing and gave Kaisen a serious look.

"I'm not sure? Has she said anything to you? Does she know about Andeka?" Kaisen started to pace in front of Harper.

"She hasn't said anything. David told us not to say anything so I haven't."

"Well if she can use your powers than she has to know. You can't use it if you don't know it exists. And if she can use yours, than that means she is a Shaire, like David. This is crazy." Kaisen said then he stopped pacing, turned towards Harper and smiled. "She likes me."

"What?" Harper asked, making a funny face. "How do you know that?"

"She used my powers to pull me in, we almost kissed. I thought I was doing it at first but then I stopped, I didn't want her to do something out of her control but she took over the power." Kaisen said. "I have never felt anyone do that before." Harper slugged Kaisen in the arm and shook his head.

"Well that is great for you brother, but we need to make sure what you thought happened, actually happened."

"You said it yourself, she froze the accident."

"Yes, but she hasn't brought it up. I have done many things that she should be able to catch on to, but it seems like she doesn't notice what is happening."

"I have an idea. I will give you three minutes, go in there and try to convince Charlotte that she can win Monopoly. I will open my power to her and see if she uses them. If she wins, she used it, if I win, then it was a hoax." Kaisen said as he started to walk off. "Three minutes, Harper." He reminded, disappearing around the corner.

I COULDN'T GET Kaisen out of my head; I heard footsteps walking back to the room, my heart started to pound as I waited for Kaisen to walk back into the room, but instead Harper walked in.

"I feel better." He announced, looking around for his brother. "Where's Kaisen?"

"I don't know, I think he went to the bathroom, too." I said.

"Well, whose turn is it?" Harper asked.

"It's yours."

"I'm going to lose, Kaisen is just way too lucky." Maybe Kaisen is a Brink. I remember that type of Cigam has overwhelming luck. And after finding my name in the book under my father's name and somehow pausing the accident, I couldn't help but wonder what gift I have, too.

"I know, I don't stand a chance, we better just quit now." I said, trying to get Harper to say anything about Cigam powers.

“No way!” Harper demanded. “We need to make him lose, he always wins. Don't worry you can do it. Just concentrate on winning. Here, when he gets back, I’ll trade you, my good land for some of your bad land, so you can put houses down on your properties. I will distract him while you concentrate on winning so he won't be paying attention. I’m the banker so I will lend you some cash now. He will never know.”

“You want me to win? I don’t know if that’s such a good idea. I don’t do well at winning.”

“You’ll be fine, I’ll help you. Don’t worry.” Harper encouraged. “I think I can hear him coming down the hall. Just play it cool. Don’t give our secret away.” He said, winking at me when Kaisen walked in. “What took you so long? It’s your turn.”

We started the game back up, both Harper and I concentrating hard. Kaisen didn’t seem to notice, he was still on his winning streak, but that ended after a few turns. I concentrated, maybe I could use whatever power I had to win this game. I landed on and bought all the properties on one entire side of the board and half the properties on another side. I traded board walk for two green properties from Kaisen. He had Park Place, but I wasn’t too worried. I usually skipped right over those ones, that’s the reason I didn’t own both anyways. Together, Harper and I owned all the railroads, and eventually Harper ran out of cash and had to give me his share. This game became fun after I started to win. But once Harper got down to the last of his properties, Kaisen started to catch on.

“You never go out first, what are you doing?” Kaisen accused.

"Just unlucky today I guess." Harper said trying not to smile. Kaisen glared at him and looked at me; I pulled my smile down as far as I could.

Harper went out. Then it was a battle between me and Kaisen. He played hard, placing hotels on all of his property, which wasn't near as much as I had. I couldn't put hotels on everything though, I didn't have enough money. I kept track of what Kaisen landed on the most and put hotels on those places and put houses on most of the others. I was quite proud of myself for making it this far, despite the help from Harper. Kaisen had thirty three dollars left and he was coming up to my side of the board. He had to roll a five to land on a chance and another ten to get out of my money trap without going broke. His first roll was snake eyes. That meant he landed on a hotel space and paid all his money plus a few properties, he then had to roll again because he rolled a double. He got a five. Then he knew he was done for. He was only in the middle of my side of the board when he had utilities and four other properties left. He had to sell his hotels for money, so he could pay me. His properties were almost useless now. The only thing worth anything was his utilities, which I planned to take next. In the end, he put up a good fight and tried to trade just enough to get by. It didn't work. He was a good sport though; he never complained or gave up. He did lose though. He landed on jail, and I kept going passed 'go,' collected two hundred dollars, and waited for him to get out of jail, which led him straight to the expensive hotels. He landed on the most expensive and had to mortgage all of his properties he had left and that didn't even cover half the cost. When we were done, Harper tried to cover his laugh with a cough, which didn't work.

"You sneaky troll, you set me up." Kaisen barked at Harper and gave him a weird smile.

"Hey, it's not my fault you lost to a girl." Harper exclaimed, they exchanged a strange look and then burst into laughter.

"Hey, thanks a lot. I win and you insult me." I jokingly complained at him.

"You cheaters." Kaisen said laughing and jumped up trying to tackle Harper. Harper dodged him and ran from the room into the darkness of the long hall. Kaisen ran outside the door after Harper.

I WAS ALL alone in the game room and started to pick up the game when I heard a noise. I looked up and Kaisen was standing in the doorway smirking at me.

"I can't believe you cheated." He said still smiling, but walking towards me.

"You win all the time. It was my turn. Plus, I didn't cheat." I said.

"Whatever. I win because I am good and I play fair. That doesn't count; you guys double teamed me. That is cheating." He raised his eye brows, still walking towards me.

"Are you sure you don't cheat? Because you win an awful lot." I teased, probably telling him that I knew more than anyone thought. If I could tell someone what I know it would be him and Harper. "It was my turn to win." I stuck my tongue out at him.

"Don't stick your tongue out at me." He said. I jumped up and ran to the other side of a table. I stuck out my tongue at him again.

"What are you going to do about it?" I challenged. He lunged at me, but I moved out of the way. I ran around the table and over to the door. I turned to see where he was and he was fast on my heels and before I could move out of the way, he ran into me, knocking us both to the floor. We both laughed as we lied on the floor. Kaisen had landed half on top of me and when I looked up at him my face was two inches from his. I could hear his breathing now, hard and jagged.

"Sorry." He laughed as he moved a few inches away but didn't move far enough. I could smell his cologne from his chest, he smelled so good. I sat up on my elbows towards him, not fully aware of what I was doing. My hand moved forward on the floor bracing me as I leaned. Kaisen started to move and his hand brushed against mine and he left it there, touching mine. I bit the edge of my lip, something I did when I was nervous or just turned on. I noticed he was leaning in as well. Just as I was about to lean in more, a voice came from the hall. It was Harper, coming back from where ever he had been. I wish he would go away. Kaisen sighed and then rolled off of me onto his back next to me. Harper gave us a strange look when he came into the room.

"What were you two doing?" He asked in an accusing but joking tone. Kaisen ignored him as he climbed to his feet then extended his hand to help me up. "It's almost two in the morning." Harper said as he read his phone.

"It's really late; I'm going to bed, good night." I said walking out of the room fast, not looking back. That was a very awkward moment, but I loved every minute of it. It was exhilarating. Once I got back to my room I hopped into bed and tried to sleep. It was a failed attempt.

"She did it again. And she said I win a lot. It was weird how she said it though, it seemed like she was accusing me of something." Kaisen said. "Do you think she knows she did it?"

"I'm not sure." Harper said. "I told her to concentrate and think about winning, she didn't seem like she knew what was going on."

"Either way, we still aren't sure if she knows, so you can't say anything. She has to bring it up first." Kaisen said and Harper agreed.

THE SUN STARTED TO shine in my window when I finally drifted into unconsciousness. I woke up to a knock at my door.

"Come in," I mumbled loudly to the annoying sound. I didn't even open my eyes to see who was there.

"Good morning, honey, do you want to come down for breakfast? It's nine-thirty." It was Marilyn. She glided softly to me and sat down on the edge of my bed.

"Where is my dad?" I asked, still half asleep. I sat up and rubbed the sleep from my eyes.

"He had to go take care of some business; he will be home in a few days. Are you hungry?"

"Yeah, I'll be right down. Are the boys awake yet?"

"No, I'm on my way to their rooms right now. They don't usually sleep this long, were you guys up late?"

"Yeah," I yawned, "we ended our monopoly game around two this morning."

"Oh, well, if you're still tired, Chef Mallow can put your breakfast in the fridge until you wake up." She told me.

"I don't think I can sleep any more. I might take a nap later. Besides, I'm too hungry to sleep. I'll meet you down stairs."

"Alright," She said, gently rising off the bed and closing the door behind her.

After breakfast I went back to my room, locked the door and pulled out the Cigam Family History books from under my bed. I opened them up and started reading. The one from my family didn't say anything useful. I was curious about what my gift might be. I read maybe ten pages when I fell asleep and had the strangest dream. I was standing in the field behind the maze, next to the pond. I watched from behind a young woman as she raised her hands up into the air and before I could wonder what she was doing I saw it. The storm clouds exploded out of nowhere and they grew over the pond. The clouds became dark and the wind started to blow and lightning was touching the earth with such force that the ground would shoot up dirt into the sky. As I watched the weather change by the woman I noticed a mob of people across the field charging towards her. I looked around and no one else was there to protect her. She was all alone, except for me. Then as the mob grew nearer, the ground started to shake, and the woman moved her hands towards the earth as if to pull large mounds out of the ground. The mob of people came closer and closer. The woman picked off a few people one by one with the storm and by splitting the earth, but there were too many people. A man ran up to the young woman and pulled a knife out and stabbed her. He caught her as she fell and laid her down in the grass, then before my eyes the mob vanished and the storm evaporated. Once everyone except the man and woman were gone, I ran up to them. The man laid the woman down in the grass, stood up and looked at me. It was Kaisen, he gazed into my eyes and then he turned around and disappeared just like the mob had. I ran to the woman and knelt down next to her. I pulled her hair away from her face and froze. The young woman was me.

I WOKE UP SWEATING and confused. I have had strange dreams before but nothing like this. Maybe it was a sign. I really started to like Kaisen as much more than a friend. Was my subconscious trying to tell me that he is dangerous? …no… that is stupid; people have crazy dreams like this all the time. I shook my head until it was cleared and glanced at my clock. I had only slept a few hours, but it was nearly time for lunch. I went to the bathroom and splashed water on my face before heading downstairs to eat.

When I got down to the dining room Kaisen was already seated, in his normal spot across from my normal spot. I tried to not make eye contact with him. Then I started to feel ridiculous. I sat down in my usual place. Harper was sitting at the end of the table where my dad usually sits.

"Where is Marilyn?" I asked.

"She had to run some errands; she will be back for supper, though." Harper answered as he gulped down his glass of water.

Chef Mallow brought us our food but I couldn't eat much. My dream was bothering me. I started to think about what I did in the dream and then wanted to know more about who I am, what my powers are and why everyone has kept Andeka a secret from me. I have known now for about six months. I have learned as much as I can from the books. But I need answers and I think that today is the perfect day to ask... if I have the courage to ask. With Dad and Marilyn gone I can ask Kaisen and Harper without getting into trouble. I took a deep breath and thought about what I wanted to ask. Then I thought about the few sentences of Dekia that I could try.

"Can I ask you guys a question?" I started anxiously.

"Sure? What?" Kaisen asked looking up at me.

I panicked and said, "Never mind, it's nothing." Both boys gave me a glance and went back to eating. "It's just that I had this strange dream, a kind that I have never had before and... never mind, it's stupid." I started to get hot and I couldn't wait any longer for answers, I put my hand up to my mouth and very calmly and quietly I said, "Soy que sue dum." I can't remember what that meant but it caught their attention. Kaisen started coughing and Harper kind of laughed.

"I knew it!" Harper exclaimed with a smile.

"What did you say?" Kaisen asked me.

"Nothing," I said, worried that I was in trouble.

"No, you said something, what was it?" Kaisen asked again, he glanced at Harper who was beaming at me.

"I, I don't know what I said." I confessed.

"She said what you think it was that she said." Harper announced with a smile. "Soy que sue dum." He copied my words and then laughed. Kaisen laughed a little, too.

"Who taught you that?" Kaisen asked me.

"No one, I found it in a book."

"A dictionary?"

"No, a history book." I said.

"Which one?" Kaisen asked.

"I found two history books and then two dictionaries and then a history and prophecies book." I said calmly.

"I'm impressed that you found it all, but a little disappointed that you didn't find it sooner." Harper said.

"I found it over the summer, but at first I didn't think it was real, but I kept reading and studying. Then one day I just knew, I guess. I didn't want to say anything around my dad or Marilyn. I didn't know if I was supposed to find out."

"We wanted to tell you but we couldn't say anything until you were more comfortable here." Kaisen explained.

"How much of the language do you know?" Harper beamed.

"Not much, just a few sentences that I memorized." I said.

"Like what?" Harper's eyes got big and he leaned over the table at me. I took a minute to think and then I carefully tried to pronounce the few other things I remembered.

"Boy ster ung… uh… Tay grump shay." I said as Harper laughed at my last comment. "What did I say?"

"Well that's a good sign, you're saying things and you don't know what they mean?" Kaisen laughed with sarcasm. His smile made my heart flutter.

"Soy que sue dam means I eat love soup, but if you say soy day sue dum it means I love you. Boy ster ung means repeat what you said, and Tay grump shay means your crickets out." Harper translated confused. "I think you meant Que grum tay. It means that's good."

"Oh, okay." I said, embarrassed.

"What else do you know, and I don't mean the language." Kaisen asked.

"Mostly… everything, I think." I said. "I have been reading and trying to learn all I can about all of this. I think it's fascinating."

"When did you say you found out about all of this?" Harper asked.

"Over the summer, do you remember when we went fishing?" I asked. Harper nodded. "Well I noticed that you didn't walk up to get me to throw me in the water. There were only one set of wet foot prints on the deck and they were from you carrying me back to the water. I started to read more and memorize things after that."

"Nice." Harper exclaims. "I tried to do things like that around you so you might catch me and I would have to tell you, but everything was very subtle."

"So that means that Jess and Connor know?" I asked. "You did that while they were there."

"Yeah, they are Cigam as well." He said.

"Hey Charlotte, will you go get the history books and the prophecy book?" Kaisen asked with a smile. I smiled back and went upstairs. I was finally going to get answers, I thought to myself. When I came back down I heard them talking.

"I told you that she paused the accident." Harper said in a quiet tone. I walked in, pretending that I didn't hear anything. They dropped the conversation when I walked in and set the books down on the table. I was officially done with lunch; I was too excited to eat anything else. I wanted to know everything. The thought of another world and magic powers was so astonishing and mind blowing. I knew it, Andeka was real but having Kaisen and Harper confirm that it exists makes it more real.

We finished lunch and opened up the books on the table. I couldn't stop thinking about what 'gifts or powers' Kaisen and Harper had. I had so many questions.

Chapter 8

"I DON'T REALLY know how to start. I don't know how much you know." Kaisen said while Harper walked out of the room.

"I think I know a lot, just start at the beginning, I' m fine with hearing the information twice." I said with a smile. Kaisen smiled back at me.

"This book probably tells you that the treaty locked the two worlds from anyone coming or going between them, but the worlds were unlocked about two hundred years ago. So now cigam can travel between the two worlds freely." Kaisen tells me.

"And humans can too?" I asked.

"Well they would be able to if they knew about Andeka, but you can only travel into Andeka if you know it exists. And even though there are many ways to get out of Andeka, none of the creatures in Andeka can get out either, unless a cigam lets them out." Kaisen explains.

"Do Cigam live in the human world or stay in Andeka?"

"A lot of Cigam live in Andeka but some cigam live outside now because there was an incident about 17 years ago, when Balano-Regelnin King, Bala for short, tried to take over Andeka and assassinate the rulers of the four territories. He was sent to Zweb: an isolation jail, you could call it. He has broken out twice, in the last three years, but he was caught both times, not even a mile away. The Cigam that controls Zweb have been contouring it to Bala's gift, so that he can't escape again. A lot of Cigam moved to other parts of the human world after that. Bala King tried to destroy a lot of the Cigam so he could be the last one. He wants to destroy Andeka's kingdoms and take the thrown as Andeka's supreme ruler and eventually the human world as well."

"That's a lot of territory for one person to handle alone." I joked.

"Yeah," Kaisen laughed, his seductive grin unhinging from the corner of his mouth. I got the chills.

"So what is your gift?" I ask.

"I am a Cigam-Loss; I have the ability to persuade someone to feel or think a certain way." He said. "Here let me show you." He held out his hand to me, so I placed my hand in his. My emotions run wild inside me. As I place my hand in his my heart jumps and my blood boils. Then I start to feel different things. First happiness, then fear, then shyness, and it continued to change until I noticed him looking at me. We both looked at each other for a long second. I can't look away; maybe he is persuading my mind to keep eye contact. Then I notice his large brown eyes have a small ring of caramel around the center and his lips are parted and I feel them call to me. Kiss me. Kiss me! Kiss me!

Come closer. I think to myself. Lean in closer so I can reach. His smile faded as he stared at my face, leaning in a little bit. I moved in also. My eyes moved from his eyes to his lips. They were so perfectly curved and plump. My eyes reconnected with his, as our faces were only inches away now. I pulled my lips into a soft pucker, leaning in a tad more. I could hear a little voice in my head telling me to push forward and let our lips touch. I couldn't tell if that was his voice or mine, but I didn't care. Just then, I saw something flicker in my peripheral vision, and I automatically pulled away. Kaisen dropped my hand. I instantly felt my own emotions again. I felt a little awkward again.

"Don't stop on my account," Harper joked, making me jump.

I didn't know what to say or do. I looked back at Kaisen. He was glaring at Harper.

"Don't worry, I won't tell." Harper smiled.

"There is nothing to tell, nothing happened." Kaisen frowned. "I was just showing her how my powers work." He tried to explain.

"Seduction. Nice."

"Shut up, Harper." Kaisen said as he rolled his eyes. "I'll be right back." He said as he pulled out his phone and left the room.

"I think you made him mad, where did he go?" I asked.

"I'm not sure, but I think he is trying to persuade me to take you somewhere, but I don't know where. He went to call someone, I think." He stared off into space, trying to figure out what Kaisen wanted.

"What is your gift?" I asked Harper, bringing him down from space.

"I'm a Cigam-Bain. I can transport places. I have been practicing and can take someone with me. Only one though, once we graduate, I'll start college and learn a bunch of different stuff. I really want to get a job as a traveler. I want to get good enough where I can work for one of the rulers of Andeka and transport them from place to place, except I don't want to work for Kaisen."

"Why would you work for Kaisen?" I asked.

"How much did Kaisen tell you?"

"Not much." I told him. "Why?"

"There are four kingdoms of Andeka."

"I know that."

"When your dad and my mom got married they each ruled their own kingdom. Now they combined it into one larger kingdom, but when they hand it down to the oldest child, they are planning to split them again. Charlotte, you are heir to your father's Kingdom." It took a few seconds to register.

"What?" I asked. "Holy sh..."I finished my cuss word silently.

Kaisen came back into my room with two jackets over his arm. "Grab a jacket; it's going to get cold tonight."

"What did you do to Charlotte?" He asked, staring at me.

"I told her about her lineage." Harper half smiled.

"I'm fine. It's just a lot to take in, right now." I said.

“It won't be so bad Charlotte; you have many, many years of training before you will inherit anything.” He told me, and then turned to Harper. “Will you please take us to the Darby’s house?” Harper looked confused, again. “It will be easier to explain if we just show her some things that go on here.” Kaisen explained.

“All right, I will take you first to show her what to do.” Harper told Kaisen, and then turned to me. “Pay close attention, this isn’t the easiest thing to do, but it’s the fastest way to get places. I am a Bain, I can travel quickly. I will have to come back for you. Put on your jacket, it will be easier to travel if you don’t have to hold on to a lot of things.” Harper tried to explain what he was about to do, I watched in amazement as Kaisen stood very still, Harper placed his arms on Kaisen’s shoulders and took a deep breath. Before Harper could exhale, they were both gone. They just disappeared. I waited as patiently as I could for Harper to come back for me. Two minutes seemed liked an hour. Then, Harper reappeared. “See, no problem. It will go by quickly and it doesn’t hurt, either.” Harper tried to reassure me; maybe something on my face told him I was scared. “Stand very still, just like Kaisen did.” Harper came over to me and began to put his arms around me and I couldn’t stay still. I could feel what he felt, like I was channeling Kaisen's powers. “It might be easier if you just hold on, too. Since it’s your first time in travel I am going to hold on to you, you might move too much, I wouldn’t want to let go.”

“Oh, great, that makes me feel loads better.” I said anxiously.

“Just hold on to me. You’ll be fine.”

I did as he told me. He took a deep breath and so did I. I closed my eyes tight. Not even a second later Harper cleared his voice and I opened my eyes. I was standing on the side of a road, still in Harper's arms. I didn't know if I could let go yet. I looked around and saw Kaisen waiting for us.

"That was weird, we were in my room and now I'm... Where am I?" I said as I let go of Harper and we walked over to Kaisen.

"This is the entrance to Andeka. We have to cross into Andeka to get to the Darby's house." Kaisen explained.

"Why didn't we go straight there? Why did we stop here?"

"I can't travel between worlds, yet. I can only travel within the world I start in. We have to pass through that tunnel," Harper pointed to an old looking tunnel not even 10 feet wide.

We walked towards the tunnel; I wondered how different Andeka would be from here. When I went to the Darby's house before, I didn't notice this tunnel, and it looked like a normal place, I hadn't noticed anything different. We passed through the tunnel with no problem; we just walked straight through it. It wasn't what I was expecting at all. Andeka looked exactly like Europe, nothing really had changed. It just looked like we were on the other side of the tunnel. I don't really know what I was expecting, but it wasn't this. The book made Andeka seem like an amazing and different place to be. It was kind of disappointing.

"Now that you know what to do, I'll take you first, so you don't have to stand in the middle of nowhere by yourself." Harper explained, walking towards me, stopping directly in front of me. I kind of wished that Kaisen was the one I had to put my arms around, but I'm glad I was in a close enough friendship with Harper for this not to be awkward at all. So, again, I held on tight, closed my eyes and took a deep breath.

"You can let go now," Harper said. I opened my eyes and I was standing at the Darby's front porch.

"Sorry, I didn't realize we had gone already." I replied.

"You should really keep your eyes open when we travel again, it looks really sweet." Harper said right before he disappeared and reappeared.

"Harper you're getting pretty fast, I just talked to Kaisen a few minutes ago, and you had to bring two people and stop in between." Connor Darby said when he answered the door.

"I know, I would be faster but I haven't been able to practice much in the house." He explained, hiking his thumb over his shoulder, referring to me.

"So, are Bubba and Harriett here yet?" Kaisen asked as he pushed himself into the large house. I didn't realize that Harper had gone and come back already.

"They are on their way." He answered.

When Bubba and Harriett arrived, we all sat around the Darby's living room. Kaisen explained what had happened during lunch, and how he thought it would be easier for me to understand if they show me how some of their talents work. Harriet went first. She can calm people's moods.

Harriett started by standing in front of me, placed her hand on my shoulder and instantly my mood changed. I felt relaxed, like I had just taken very strong pain medications that numbed my whole body. I couldn't even speak I was so calm. I felt weaker, like I was tired, and slowly I just relaxed enough that I could no longer hold my eyes open and I fell asleep.

"Charlotte, Charlotte." A deep but gentle voice was calling. I felt a warm hand on my neck and then my head shook. "Wake up, Charlotte."

As I opened my eyes, I saw Kaisen pull his hand from my neck and he straightened up in his seat next to me.

"Whoa, how long was I out?" I asked embarrassed that I had fallen asleep.

"Not long, are you okay?" Kaisen asked.

"Yeah, what did she do to me?"

"She relaxed you a little too much and you passed out." Harper said laughing.

"Does that happen a lot or is it just me?" I hoped it was normal to fall asleep when she used her gift on people, I didn't want to be the only one.

"Sorry, I pushed it on you too hard, I didn't know I could make someone so calm that they passed out, I thought I killed you for a second." Harriett said with a distressed look on her face.

"Its fine, it didn't hurt." I reassured her.

Connor and Jessie are twins and have the same talent, which was "Vou," or to agree. It is similar to Kaisen, but it just makes people see their side. They can't persuade someone to do anything other than to take sides. Bubba is a Dau, someone with health. He offered to cut his hand with a knife so I could see him heal it, but I told him I believed him.

Once everyone was done demonstrating and telling me about their talents, they let me ask any questions I had. I had so many I wasn't sure where to start.

"So, you guys aren't allowed to use your talents at school?"

"Definitely not, most Cigam gifts are subtle enough that normal people don't recognize it, but we still have to be careful." Harriett explained.

"How does everyone do it? Like if I had a gift how would I use it?" I was really curious about this question.

"You do have a gift, Charlotte. You are a Cigam, also." Harper said.

"What kind of Cigam am I?" I asked.

"Well most Cigam follow a family member's power. Since your dad is your only Cigam parent, you are probably a Cigam-Shaire. It means that you can use any power of a cigam that you have come into contact with." Kaisen explained. "You have to master each skill that you acquire. It may sound overwhelming or complicated but really it's not that hard to figure out."

"So since you all have different gifts, I should be able to use each of them?"

"Sure. Did you want to try one?"

"And how do I do that?" I asked.

"Come here, I'll show you." Harriett said. "Since I calm people's moods, it should be pretty easy for you to do it; the basics are easy to learn. Bubba, come be our dummy, please." He came over to us and stood in front of me while Harriett put her hands on my shoulders from behind me. "Now Charlotte, I want you to take a deep breath and clear your mind. Think about something calming, like how you feel if you were lying on the beach watching a sunset and there was nothing bad in the world." I did as she told me, trying to clear my mind and be calm. "Okay, I want you to hold Bubba's face in your hands, but don't do anything yet." I did as she told me. "Now, close your eyes and concentrate, try to make Bubba calm. Just imagine him sleeping, try to make him fall asleep." I tried to concentrate but it was hard, I wasn't sure exactly how I was supposed to make him calm by just thinking about it. I stood there for a few seconds, which felt like minutes. "Bubba, do you feel anything?"

"No, not yet."

"Concentrate harder Charlotte. Think about something peaceful, it's really that simple." Harriett said.

"Still nothing." Bubba said.

"Harper, could you make him upset please."

"My pleasure." Harper smiled. He walked over to Bubba and whispered something in his ear. I felt Bubba's emotions change instantly. Whatever Harper told him made him quite mad.

"Good. Now, Charlotte, try harder."

I imagined Bubba feeling the same way I did when Harriett calmed me earlier. I imagined him closing his eyes and falling asleep.

"She did it, I feel somewhat better. It's not as calm as Harriet can do, but I can definitely tell something changed." Bubba said after a few more seconds of concentration.

"So does that mean I am a Shaire like my father?" I asked feeling accomplished.

"I guess it does." Harriett smiled at me, "good job."

HARPER TOOK ME TO the tunnel to leave Andeka first. I stood very still as he wrapped his arms around me like before. I took a deep breath, this time I knew when we were there because the noise around us changed. It went from Kaisen and Harriett talking, to a faint snarling sound. I opened my eyes and looked around for the source of the noise.

"Shh… don't make any noises." Harper whispered to me as he held a finger up to his lips. He then pointed to two small dark brown objects fighting. They were only about 12 feet away.

"What are those things?" I asked, trying to be quite.

"They are Dernips. They shouldn't hurt you as long as you don't get their attention, I will be right back."

"No, please don't leave me here alone." I pleaded, but before I could say anything else, Harper was gone. I stood very still, watching the two large mole-like creatures. They had long yellow nails on their front paws, and their teeth were the same shade of yellow and looked just as sharp. A loud screeching noise came from one of the dernips and it whimpered as it hobbled away. The other dernip started sniffing the ground around him, keeping his nose to the ground it zigzagged among the trees and grass, getting closer to me as it walked. It was only a few feet away when I sucked in a deep breath and it heard me. Its red eyes beamed up at me and it stretched its arms and talons out and started to charge.

"Charlotte, come on." Kaisen said grabbing my hand and pulling me towards the tunnel. "Don't worry; it can't get out of Andeka unless a Cigam lets it out."

"Those things are hideous. Did you see its claws and teeth?" I asked, still amazed at the weird creature. I felt Kaisen's warm hand under mine and then when I started to feel his emotions, he dropped my hand. I wondered if he could feel my emotions too.

"We saw it." Harper said as he laughed at me. He didn't look concerned about the weird animal, but I had never seen anything like it. Thinking back to the accident, I wasn't quite sure what that was either.

"Harper, I never asked before, but what animal did we hit in the accident?" They both glanced at each other and back at me.

"I'm surprised you didn't ask before now, it was a Rhintyl. An animal close to a moose but smaller. It is very rare to hit them on the road; something must have scared it because normally it is deeper in the forest." Harper answered.

"So we were in Andeka during the accident?" I wondered.

"Yes, we had just passed over the line between worlds when it ran across the road." He told me before he transported me back to the house. "I think that is why you were able to pause the accident, because it's easier to use our powers in Andeka." I started to think about what other possibilities I have with these powers.

"What other things do you think I can do?" I asked.

"You can do anything that anyone around you can do. That is the limit to your powers. A Shaire can only use the powers that are around them." Kaisen said.

"Then how could I stop the accident?"

"Harper told me about that, I think it was probably when you learned about Andeka, you started lifting powers from the Cigam around you even though you didn't know you were doing it. You probably used what you accidentally stored when you were in the moment of the crash. When adrenaline is pumping it is much easier for a young Cigam to use their powers." When we got inside the house Harper disappeared into the kitchen. Kaisen turned to me. "Why didn't you tell me before that you knew? We talked almost every day since the accident and you knew the whole time?"

"I found the book a few weeks before school started. I assumed no one wanted me to know and I didn't want anyone to take the books away from me before I figured it out."

"You can tell me anything; I wouldn't have told anyone if you didn't want me to." He said sweetly. I looked into his beautiful brown eyes, he was telling the truth. It crossed my mind a few times to ask him about it, but I never got the courage.

"I know, I wanted to tell someone, but I guess I am really good at keeping secrets." I smiled. He grinned back at me practically taking my breath away. Damn, he was so gorgeous. Harper walked back into the room before I could think anything more inappropriate than I already was.

"Charlotte, do you want to practice your powers with me?" Harper asked. "You could try to use Kaisen's powers on me. Come on, it will be fun." He grabbed my hand and pulled me towards the staircase, Kaisen followed. When we got up stairs we sat on the couch in the game room, me in the middle, the boys on opposite sides of me.

"What do I do first?" I asked nervously.

"Close your eyes and clear your mind." Kaisen started. I did as he told me. "Now, take Harper's hands in yours.

Concentrate on what I tell you okay." He leaned down and whispered in my ear, "*Make him want a sandwich.*" Then he placed his hand on my arm. I thought carefully at what Harper should want. I couldn't do much because I kept remembering that Kaisen's warm hand was on my arm, but I tried really hard. Then I started to feel Kaisen's emotions again. I tried to push them from my mind and only focus on Harper. I started to feel Harper's emotions and then I tried to change them. After a few minutes Kaisen asked Harper if he felt anything. He said he didn't notice anything different. "Try harder, Char, make him want what I told you." I concentrated as hard as I could, thinking about Harper wanting a sandwich. After a few more minutes Kaisen stopped me. "Do you feel anything yet Harper?"

"Nope, this is more boring that I thought, do you care if we take a break?" Harper asked me, I shook my head and he left the room.

"Why can't I do it?"

"I don't know. You have used my powers before and you didn't even know you were doing it. Be patient, it's only your first time consciously trying, we can practice over break and you will eventually catch on to the powers around you. It will get easier I promise." Kaisen said taking my hand in his. "Plus, Harper is stubborn sometimes. He probably isn't paying as much attention as he should." We both laughed at that. Harper was someone who seems like he jokes all the time, and I like that. Kaisen jokes too but is more serious.

"Do you think I will be able to stop time, like I did during the accident?"

"It's a possibility, but I'm not sure how you did it. There was no one else around you to feed you their power to be able to do that." He said.

"Do you think...?" I started but stopped when Harper walked in the room.

"You are going to spoil dinner." He told Harper, who was carrying a plate.

"I'm sorry, I had a craving for a sandwich and I couldn't ignore it." Harper said. Kaisen started to laugh and then so did I. I did it; I made Harper want a sandwich.

"How strong were these cravings?" Kaisen asked.

"What do you mean?" Harper asked.

"Charlotte did that. She made you want a sandwich, that's what I told her to do." Kaisen answered.

Chapter 9

I INFORMED MARILYN THAT I knew about Andeka. She was actually relieved. I guess there are a lot of things that they haven't been able to do at the house while I was here because I didn't know about the powers.

"Charlotte," Marilyn started, "I forgot to tell you, but in two weeks there is an Annual Cigam Holiday Banquet we go to every year. It's a fancy dinner, with dancing, and there is always a large firework show. You don't have to dance though, actually you don't have to go at all if it's too soon, but I thought I would let you know." Marilyn rambled on like she normally did when she was excited about something.

"I would love to. It sounds like fun." I tried not to sound too enthusiastic.

"Good. Well, I guess we need to make a shopping day for us to go get dresses. Are you all right with that?" She said with excitement.

"Yeah, I can't wait. I love to dress up nice." I smiled.

"Me too, I will have to take you out more often. The boys used to go out every weekend."

"Why don't they go out anymore?"

"I'm sure Kaisen goes out back at college, but he studies a lot. Harper doesn't study at all so I'm not sure why he doesn't go out. I guess it's because Kaisen isn't around anymore. They used to go places together. I'm sure he likes spending time with his new sister. I don't think he was able to take you many places because most of the places he goes are where other Cigam are. Now that you know, I'm sure you guys will go out with friends a lot more." There was a long pause. "Well, I will make arrangements for us to get fitted for dresses. I'm so glad you want to go. There are always many cute boys there. I bet some of them will ask you to dance." She was keyed up by the time she left the room. I didn't care if I was asked to dance by anyone except Kaisen. He had only been home for a few days and, already, we got close to kissing twice. I knew I liked him when I first met him. He obviously liked me, unless I was persuading him to kiss me, which would be awkward. He was confusing because, he acted, for the most part, normal when we were hanging out with other people, but as soon as we were alone, tension brought us close. He seems shy, or scared or something.

"Is my dad back yet?" I asked worriedly, I wasn't sure how long I can hide that I know about Andeka. It's weird, I can hide the secret until I tell one person, then it seems impossible to keep it from everyone else.

"I just got off the phone with him, his plane just landed." Marilyn started. "Don't worry; he is going to be very happy that you know." She didn't sound very convincing. Marilyn told us I would tell my dad tonight at dinner that I have learned about Andeka. She said he will probably be relieved that I know. Since I am heir to my father's kingdom, the sooner I find out, the better it will be for the kingdom. The sooner I start training with my powers, the better I will become and the better I can defend my people. It is so much to take in; a few days ago I was nervous to talk to Kaisen and Harper about Andeka, now I have to learn how to run a quarter of it. This is crazy.

When David arrived back at the house I tried to stay as far away from him as possible. If I could avoid him until dinner then Marilyn would help me tell him. He caught on fast when everyone said hi and bye when he came home. Neither the boys nor I wanted to talk to David very long; just in case he knew something was up... we took the wrong approach.

"Okay, what's going on? Everyone is acting strange. What happened while I was gone?" I overheard my dad ask Marilyn before we sat down for dinner. There was a long pause like she was waiting for him to say something else.

"We were going to tell you at dinner, it's nothing bad." I heard Marilyn say from her office. She saw me walk by the door and pointed out the crack of the door at me. I tried to get away but Dad came out of the door before I could run around the corner.

"Charlotte," I turned to look at him. "Is there something going on that you would like to tell me?"

"Uh, no." I said. I could feel him try to persuade me to tell him what is going on. It was working, too. Dad gave me a look that made the persuasion even stronger.

"Charlotte, tell me." He said as his gaze caught me. He was using his powers over me. I wonder if he has done that before, I have never noticed. He is using Kaisen's powers, I wonder if Kaisen has ever used them on me.

"That's not fair. You can't just use your powers anytime you want me to tell you something." He gave me a shocked look.

"What did you just say?"

"That's what I was hiding. Over the summer, I found the books in the back of the library. I have been reading them and when you left I asked Harper and Kaisen what everything meant. They showed me what they could do and took me to Andeka, to the Darby's house. I didn't want to tell you because I thought you would be mad." I said.

"Why would I be mad? I wanted you to know about Andeka. But, I needed to let you figure it out on your own." He said.

"Oh. Why didn't you just tell me?" I asked.

"You are almost eighteen, it would have sounded like a joke and you wouldn't have believed me. I hoped you would have told me that you knew sooner. If I would have known that you knew I would have taught you some things before you started school. I am glad you know, I actually need to talk to you about college." He said.

"I know that Cigam go to colleges to learn about their powers and learn how to use their powers for their careers." I told him.

"Then you must also know that you will get my kingdom when I pass it down?"

"Yes."

"So have you decided to train to be a leader?" He asked.

"I don't know yet." I said looking down at my hands, which were now folded into each other.

"You don't have to decide now but I would like you to look into schools in Andeka and at least try to learn your powers." He said.

"I will think about it." I told him.

FOR THE NEXT TWO weeks I tried to figure out what all I was able to do with my powers. I used them every chance I got to practice. I started by clearing my mind, the number one thing everyone kept telling me to do before I started. When I couldn't clear my mind I would write down everything and anything that bothered me or that I needed to remember or needed to do. When everything was down on paper, I could clear my mind and not worry about forgetting anything. The first few weeks were easy. I managed to persuade Harper to come knock on my door a few different times. He wasn't sure why he was knocking but by the third time he was knocking, he knew I was starting to get the hang of Kaisen's gift. Harper tried to teach me to transport from one side of the house to another. It was much harder than it looked. I was only able to move from my room to the hall. Harper says it's a work in progress and that I'm learning quite quickly. Then as soon as I started getting better at my powers, it started getting harder. I wasn't able to clear my mind as easily and my powers started to diminish. Kaisen would try to help me out with persuasion; he told me it was normal for it to get harder. He said all Cigam went through this stage. It would get even harder before it got easier and this is where most Cigam quit. I found out some Cigam would live human lives because they stopped believing they could use their powers.

MARILYN AND I WERE fitted for our ball gowns, nothing more had gone on between Kaisen and I. And he acted like nothing had even happened; he avoided being alone with me, too. It was strange though, because Harper had even told me Kaisen liked me, and it was obviously true if he was the one leaning in for a kiss. I hoped he would ask me to dance at the banquet or maybe other boys would ask and would make Kaisen want to make a move before anyone else did.

Marilyn's dress was very elegant but sexy at the same time; it was a navy blue form fitting dress with a long slit down the side to show some leg. It had a V-neck in the front and in the back, and the dress touched the floor.

My dress was black, it was plain but beautiful. It was form fitted around the waist and long like Marilyn's but it was off the shoulder, didn't have a slit and wasn't as tight. It had an empire waist with a V-neck which met in the middle with a diamond studded design.

The night of the banquet, Marilyn and I had matching jewelry: pearl necklace, bracelet and earrings. I also wore the emerald ring that Dad's mother gave me.

"Wow, you ladies look beautiful." Dad said as he walked into his room, where Marilyn and I were getting ready.

"Thanks hon, you don't look bad yourself." Marilyn said as I noticed he was wearing a tuxedo. I guess I didn't know how fancy this banquet would actually be, must be a pretty big deal if the men were wearing tuxes. Dad escorted Marilyn out of the room by the arm. I followed them out into the hall, down the stairs. Harper and Kaisen were waiting in the living room for us. They were wearing the same kind of Tuxedos that Dad was wearing. Kaisen was so gorgeous; he could really pull off anything he wore. He was staring at me as I came into the room, I smiled at him and he diverted his eyes to the ground and half smiled.

"Ready to go?" Harper asked us. Dad nodded and he led us out of the house. "You clean up nicely, Charlotte." Harper said as we walked outside.

"Thank you, you both look very handsome." I said as I looked to Kaisen.

"Thank you." Kaisen smiled. "Ow," he said as I glanced over to the boys just in time to see Harper elbow Kaisen in the ribs and give him a dirty look. "I mean, you look very beautiful, Charlotte." I think we both blushed at the same time. Harper rolled his eyes at us and got into the vehicle.

We rode in a limo to the castle. The castle was huge. It was four stories high and probably had forty windows facing the road. There were many people here; we were greeted by the hosts. Every year a different ruler hosts the banquet at this location. This year it was Yanie and Maerganna Hergovaben, they are the youngest of the rulers. Maerganna is pregnant with their first child and is due in two months. They were the youngest Cigam to become rulers of Andeka. The kingdom was passed down to Yanie seventeen years ago when he was just eighteen years old. Most rulers don't take over the throne until late thirties early forties, some don't even get the throne until they are in their fifties. It just depends when the current rulers want to pass down the kingdom.

After we ate, David introduced me to a few friends of the family; they had children around the same age as me. Lex and Luica Trechner both had blonde hair and blue eyes. Luica was tall and thin and her fingers were deathly skinny, when I shook her cold hand I felt like her fingers were so fragile that they might break off. Lex was a few inches taller than his sister, but with the same skinny frame.

"Would you like to dance?" Lex asked me, he was kind of cute, I don't see why not.

"Sure," I said. He took my hand and walked me to the dance floor. His hands were less bony than his sisters but still quite thin. He pulled me in, placing his left hand on my lower back and taking my left hand in his right. We lead us around the dance floor slowly.

"You are a wonderful dancer." He complimented, even though he was doing all the work. I didn't know what I was doing, I just moved along with him.

"I'm only good because my leader is a good dancer." I complimented.

"You are very beautiful, as well." He said with a smile.

"Thank you." I said. The longer we danced the creepier this guy got. He stared at me and made me feel self-conscious and strange. I hoped the song would be over soon. I regret complimenting him now; hopefully he didn't take that the wrong way. As we danced I tried not to look at Lex so I looked passed his head and as we spun around the dance floor I saw

Kaisen standing in the corner of the ballroom. I couldn't tell if he was looking at me or someone else, but my stomach turned over as I watched him all alone. As we continued dancing in circles, I tried to watch Kaisen, I looked away as my back was turned away from him, then when I was able to see the spot where he was standing he was gone. I scanned the area for him, but he was nowhere in sight. I heard the music slow to an end.

"Thank you for the dance." I said, hoping he wouldn't ask me to dance again.

"No. Thank you." He said, taking my hand and lifting it to his lips for a kiss. I gave him as real a smile as I could before I walked away. I saw Marilyn and my dad talking with some gentleman on the outside of the dance floor, but still didn't see Kaisen or Harper.

"Hey, Charlotte, would you dance with me?" A familiar voice asked. Harper was standing with his hand out towards me, hoping I would take it. "Please say yes, I asked that girl over there in the green dress and she turned me down." I tried to hold back a laugh as I took his hand.

"Of course I'll dance with you." I said. I had no problem dancing with Harper; we had gotten so close this past semester at school, and being around him at the house all the time, he had turned into my best friend.

"Maybe you'll make her jealous and she'll want to dance with me." He said with a smile.

"Oh, I see, I'm part of your evil plan to get girls." I said jokingly as he led me around the dance floor.

"Well, yeah, kind of." He laughed.

"Thanks." I said sarcastically.

"Can I ask you something?" His smile faded slightly.

"Yeah, what's up?"

"Umh, you do like Kaisen right?" He asked. I didn't know what to say. I wanted to tell the truth but was afraid to.

"He likes you, but he doesn't know if you like him back…" he started. "He didn't ask me to ask you, I'm just curious."

"Yeah, I do like him. Are you sure he likes me? He has been acting strange since he got back for the holidays."

"He definitely likes you, he is afraid you only like him as a friend or a step-brother. And he easily persuades people to do what he wants. He wasn't sure if you liked him or he was persuading you to like him. I think that's why he is afraid to make a move; he doesn't want to force you to like him."

"I guess that makes sense. I do like him though. Can I tell you something?" I said as the song stopped and another started.

"Sure."

"This may sound corny, but I felt an instant connection with Kaisen when I first met him." I wasn't done talking so we just kept dancing and as I looked up at Harper I saw Kaisen in the corner of my eye. He was dancing with a girl in a blue gown twenty feet away. I instantly got jealous. "Don't tell him I said that." I said as I looked back at Harper.

Harper looked in the direction I had been looking and saw Kaisen, too. "You have nothing to worry about, he definitely likes you. He is just dancing to be sociable. Maybe he is warming up to ask you."

"I don't think so." I said in denial.

"Do you want me to tell him to ask you?"

"No, I want him to ask me on his own, not get prompted." I replied as his eyes looked up from the girl and caught mine. I couldn't breathe anymore, I felt light headed and my stomach hurt again. I smiled at him and he smiled back.

"You know, it's easier to dance if you don't hold your breath." Harper said with a smirk.

"I hadn't noticed I was still holding it." I said exhaling.

"Maybe you should ask him to dance." Harper said.

"He is dancing with someone, I can't just go over there and cut in, that's the boy's job, plus I'm dancing with you." I said.

"At this point, you're pretty much dancing with him, you can't keep your eyes off of him and you are just swaying side to side." He said as we both looked down at our feet. I *was* just swaying.

"Sorry," I muttered.

"It's alright, cheer up, I'm only kidding." He said with a smile, and then spun me, to cheer me up. I laughed as my hand came back to his, he didn't hold it. He whipped me out by my other hand then pulled me back in. Grabbing both my hands he pushed my arms and body away from his then pulled us in close, and then we spun around again. We both laughed as we did a sort of swing dance around all the other dancers, and at the end of the song he dipped me.

"That was fun," I giggled, out of breath.

"Good, well I'm thirsty now, I'm going to get something to drink, want to come?" He beamed.

"Yeah," I followed him into the dining hall where some people were sitting around their dinner tables talking.

"Are you guys having fun?" Marilyn asked us as we gulped down our water from dinner.

"Yeah, we just got done dancing. Harper is really good." I said with a smile.

"He better be, he took two years of classes." She said winking at Harper. "Have you seen Kaisen?"

Harper answered before I could put down my water. "He is dancing with girls."

"Harper," Jessie called as she walked towards us from a few tables away. "Connor and I are going to the spot; do you guys want to come with?"

"Sure, want to come Charlotte?" He asked.

"Okay," I agreed.

"Don't get into trouble." Marilyn said as we walked towards the large archway from where we entered when we arrived. We climbed the grand staircase that wrapped around the outside of the entryway of the castle. We walked down the large corridor past the beautiful windows. There were doors along the left side of the hall and windows along the right side. We kept walking until we came to a large door at the end of the hall.

"What's in there?" I asked as Jessie opened the door for us.

"You'll see." She said with a mischievous grin. One by one we walked into a large office it was twice the size of my bedroom. It had dark wood paneling that matched all the furniture in the room. There was a giant desk in the middle of the room; there were two chairs sitting in front of it and two more matching chairs off to the side of the room with a table in between them. There was another chair behind the desk. There were stuffed deer and fish mounted on the walls along with other animals that I didn't recognize.

We didn’t stay in this room for very long, we walked through it past the desk and into another door on the left wall. This room was dark; all I could see was a round table in the corner with an old style couch next to it.

“Where are we going?” I asked.

“You'll see, we are almost there.” Harper whispered.

Jessie walked over to the window, which was our only source of light. She opened it up and climbed out. “Come on,” Jessie said motioning for us to follow her. Outside the window was a long balcony, overlooking the lit yard.

We walked all the way to the end of the balcony where a ladder covered in vines was pinned against the side of the castle, leading to the roof. Jessie hiked up her dress and started climbing. I thought she was crazy, why were we going to the roof anyways, and how are we going to get down, the boys would have no problem but I don’t think I can climb up or down a ladder with this long dress on, not to mention if I ripped the dress, Marilyn would kill me.

“I can’t go up there. I won’t be able to in this dress, and I won’t be able to get down either.” I told Harper as Connor started climbing.

“I know. I take all of the girls up there if they don't want to climb.” He asked.

“How are you going to carry me up that thing?” I asked in disbelief.

Harper just rolled his eyes, and then hugged me. As quickly as it took my eyes to refocus was as fast as it took us to get onto the roof. The quick trip took my breath away, now I know why Harper takes a deep breath before he transports. I feel like I am going to hyperventilate.

"Oh, I forgot you could do that. And I don't think I will keep my eyes open again for that." I complained. Harper just laughed at me.

"Look," Jessie said pointing to the sky above the large back yard. A beam of light came from the ground, exploding into the air in a red sun burst.

"Wow, fireworks." I said. I could almost reach them; they felt so close.

"See; is it worth it up here?" Connor asked smiling.

"Definitely!" I answered, sitting down on the roof next to Harper.

Harper's phone rang. "Hello? Yeah we are at the normal spot...yeah she is here with me. I'll be right there." He said standing up and walking to the corner of the roof.

"Where are you going? They are just starting." Jessie asked.

"I'll be right back." He said as he disappeared into thin air. I watched as the fireworks multiplied each time they burst open in the clear sky.

"Are you having fun?" Kaisen asked as he sat down beside me.

"Yes, Harper is a great dancer and the fireworks just started." I replied with a smile. He half smiled back at me, our eyes were connected, and I couldn't look away. I so badly wanted to lean in and let our lips meet, but there were people around, and I didn't want anyone to know I liked him, other than Harper, at least. Maybe he would lean in first, but he didn't; a loud noise came from the fireworks and Kaisen looked up.

"Looks like rain." Harper said as he pointed to a large black cloud in the sky.

"I hope it waits to get here until the fireworks get over, the grand finale is always the best part." Jessie stated.

The weather didn't wait for anything. While the fireworks were going on the thunder started, making it almost impossible to tell whether the noise was the thunder or the fireworks. And before the finale, it started to rain, which quickly turned into a downpour.

"Harper, can you take us inside?" Kaisen asked. Harper agreed and one by one he pulled everyone inside the dry castle: Harriett, Jessie then Connor. I felt like Harper did this on purpose, leaving Kaisen and I out in the rain together. I started to shiver when my dress was completely soaked.

"Here." Kaisen said as he took off his jacket and draped it over my shoulders. I smiled at him and he smiled back. "So much for fireworks, I don't think I can remember a time it rained during this banquet." He said. I was always at a loss for words when I was around Kaisen. I just smiled at him. "Geez, Harper, hurry up. I wonder what is taking him so long."

"Br, its freezing out here." I said, wishing he would come put his arms around me. I wasn't sure if I persuaded him with his own powers or if he wanted to, but he came over and rubbed my arms. Then thunder struck right by the balcony where we were standing, making me jump forward pushing myself into Kaisen. He didn't say anything; he just put his arms around me.

He was so warm, even though his clothes were soaked. Then without any warning, Kaisen dropped his hands and stepped back.

"Took you long enough," Kaisen said as a new set of hands hugged me from behind.

"Sorry it took so long." I could hear the smirk in Harper's tone as he took me back inside.

"Thank you." I said as Harper disappeared. The boys took much longer than it should have taken; maybe Harper was getting worn out. I took off Kaisen's soaked jacket and gave it back to him. "Thank you." I told him.

"Anytime," he said with a huge smile. "Oh, come here." He said subtly. He reached over and pulled a wet strand of hair from my face and tucked it behind my ear. "Sorry, it bugged me." He dropped his eyes slightly and kept walking down the hall next to me. I smiled at myself and could feel my cheeks warm up.

THE STORM WAS TERRIFYING. I could hear the trees outside flailing in the wind and moaning for the rain to stop. My room was constantly lit from the lightning and my whole bedroom shook from the roar of the thunder. There was no way I was going to be able to sleep in this storm. I sat up in my bed, flipped my bedside lamp on and pulled out my history book. There was no way I was going to sleep through this storm right now. I had only been reading for maybe five minutes when a knock at my door made me jump. Frightened so much by the storm, I didn't want to get out of bed long enough to see who it was, but I got up anyways. I sprinted to the door and opened it with one swift pull. It was Kaisen.

"Hey, can't sleep?" He guessed.

"Nope." I gasped for air as I swayed from getting up to fast.

"Me neither, do you want a midnight snack?" He asked as he held up a bowl of Chef Mallow's homemade puppy chow.

"Sure, come in." I opened the door for him. We sat together on the couch, separated by the bowl of food. "This is a terrible storm." I said after a flash of lightning struck close to the house followed immediately by thunder. I pulled my feet up to my chest and curled my blanket over my shoulders.

"Yeah, this is the worst one we have had in a long time." He said, popping a few pieces of food in his mouth. We sat silent for a moment, just listening to the storm. I liked being around him, I talked to him on the phone for six months and now that he is in the room with me I feel shy. That makes no sense, so I thought about what I would ask him if we were on the phone.

"Kaisen, why didn't you ask me to dance tonight?" I asked keeping my eyes on the puppy chow.

"Well I…" He stopped when lightning struck and the power went out. I screamed.

"Sorry," I said while we both laughed. "Anyways, you were saying." I said, much braver now that he couldn't see me.

"I didn't get the chance." He said.

"That's not true, you had all night." I told him.

"You were already dancing with guys; I didn't want to butt in." He said.

"Oh," I said. The lights flickered back on and he was looking at me.

"Charlotte, do you want to dance?" He asked with a smile.

"Right now?"

"Sure, why not?"

"Because I'm in my pajamas." I said. He laughed and a sexy smirk came to his lips, it made my stomach tingle.

"Oh, I see, you wanted me to ask you so you could turn me down." He laughed.

"No, I..."

"I'm just joking." He said. I laughed as I stood up to dance with him.

"What do you want to dance to?" I asked as I went over and turned my radio on.

"Something slow," He said as a slow song came onto the radio. We danced for a few seconds when a very loud ripping sound outside the window made me jump and gasp at the same time. The music stopped and the whole house went dark again. I was pressed up against Kaisen now. Oh crap. I said to myself.

"Sorry," I said out loud. Kaisen laughed.

"It's fine." I slowly released my grip on Kaisen and pulled away. "You're done dancing already? We just started."

"I don't know if you noticed but there is no music and no light."

"You don't need that to dance." I didn't protest, but let him pull me to him again and he held me as we danced to the sound of the storm.

"So, am I as good a dancer as my brother?" He asks.

"I don't know," I said in a joking tone. He made an overly exaggerated a gasp and we both laughed. He spun me around and did a few moves that Harper did while we danced. Surprisingly neither of us hit anything while we danced around my bedroom floor. We both laughed the whole time we were spinning and twirling and finally he dipped me right as the lights came back on. I watched his eyes get big. I glanced over at the table that was inches from my head.

"That was close." He said as he pulled me back to standing position and we both laughed again.

"That was fun, thank you." I said as I looked up at him. His grin turned into a smile which faded into a partial smile. He took my hand and pulled me closer to him. My heart started pounding as I watched his hand travel towards my face, he took the back side of his two first fingers and rubbed them along my cheek, and then he pulled my chin up so I would look at him. Our eyes met once again and this time we had nothing to stop us or break our gaze. He leaned down towards me in one swift movement, then stopped a few inches from my face and then looked into my eyes for any protest. He still had a hold of my hand so I pulled my arm back and his whole body shifted a step towards me and our lips met. My cheeks warmed as our lips were in sync with each other's. Kaisen released my chin and placed his hand on my lower back, pulling me into him. I wrapped my hand around the back of his neck, pulling him in closer. I couldn't breathe; my heart was beating so fast, I felt like it was going to rip right through my chest. I could feel Kaisen's heart beating just as quickly. We were now standing so close that we couldn't get any closer. Kaisen released the hand on my arm and put it around me. I pushed my hand up his arm, stopping at the top of his muscular shoulder. He pulled his arms tighter, gently lifting me off the ground then setting me back down as he loosened his grip and parted his lips from mine. Once he released me, my hands dropped to below his elbows, so I could still hold him close. We stood looking into each other's eyes for a few seconds. The tension between us built and built until I couldn't take it anymore, I pulled both of his arms towards me, hoping he would move towards me again and kiss me. And he did, right as his face came down towards mine for another kiss there was a knock at my door. We both froze and I gasped a little. We released each other and Kaisen went to sit on the couch again as I went to the door. It was Harper, of course, the same person who always walks in at the worst time.

"What are you doing?" He asked.

"Nothing, I can't sleep because of the storm," I said, trying to act natural.

"You look guilty, what are you doing in there?" He said with a sly grin.

"Nothing," I said as I opened the door a little more so he could see Kaisen. "We are eating puppy chow, do you want some?" I asked. Harper gave me a weird smile and walked in, closing the door behind him.

"How long have you guys been up?" He asked as he sat in my spot next to Kaisen.

"About a half hour, maybe," I said, sitting down across from the boys on the floor, so I could still reach the food.

"Wait a minute..." He started. Harper looked back and forth between Kaisen and me a few times. He then stared off into space a few moments. "This bowl of puppy chow is still full; it should be empty if you have been eating it for a half hour." I can't believe this, the first time he doesn't catch us doing anything and he can still tell we did something. He looks between us and raises his eye brow and smirks like the Grinch. "You two kissed...didn't you?" He accused. Kaisen and I exchanged glances quickly.

"Why do you always think we are going to kiss?" Kaisen asked calmly.

"Ah ha, you did kiss. There is no way you would stay this calm if you hadn't kissed her."

"Why not?" He asked.

"Because if you hadn't kissed her you would be paranoid that she would find out that you liked her." Kaisen and I looked at each other and laughed.

"You're weird, Harper." Kaisen said.

"Just admit it, Kaisen, you and Charlotte kissed."

"I'm not admitting anything, especially not to you." He said. A flash of lightning brightened up the whole room, and then a rumble of thunder shook the whole house very slowly as the lights flickered and went out again.

"Why does it keep doing that?" I asked rhetorically.

"Because we're in a storm." Harper says slowly and sarcastically.

"Oh, shut it, Harper. I'm going down to get something to drink; do you want to come, Charlotte?" Kaisen asked.

"Yeah," I said as my heart fluttered. The roar of the thunder made chills run down my spine. "You're beautiful when you're scared." He said as we left the room. He took my hand and walked with me downstairs.

When we got downstairs, Chef Mallow was making food in the candle lit kitchen.

"Are you guy's hungry?" He asked as Kaisen released my hand.

"Sure, what are you making?" Kaisen answered.

"I'm just cutting up some fruit to snack on until the power comes back on. The oven just preheated when the power went out. I'm making pizza." Chef Mallow replies. I sat down on a stool while Kaisen got chocolate milk for us. The power came back on shortly. We ate pizza and finished our milk. Kaisen and I got up to leave and Harper told us goodnight as he stayed down stairs with Mallow.

When we got to my door, Kaisen took my hand and kept walking until we got to his room. He opened up the door and turned on the bedside lamp.

"I should get to bed, it's late." I said, hoping that he didn't want me to stay with him in his room.

"Stay. Please." He asked sincerely. He pulled me close to him, leaned down and kissed me again. This time it was a short touch of the lips. I leaned towards him as he pulled our lips apart. I wasn't ready to end the kiss, it was too short. He backed up, pulling me with him until he got to the edge of his bed. I was really nervous, I wasn't sure how far he wanted to go, but I wasn't comfortable this close to his bed. I know I like him a lot but I wasn't ready for anything like this.

Kaisen pulled me down so my lips could meet his, and I melted. I wrapped my fingers in the back of his hair, attaching myself as best I could. He placed his hands on my lower back, lowering me down on the bed. Kaisen's lips were warm on mine as I let my lips part, parting his at the same time. Our tongues touched as my lips kept moving along with his. My heart beat faster and faster and I was gasping for breath when he pulled away breaking our lip lock.

"What's wrong?" I asked, out of breath.

"I can't breathe." He laughed and I laughed with him. "You are so beautiful." I blushed.

"So are you." I said. He smiled and tickled my side, making me flinch and bend down slightly; he pulled me over and laid me down on the bed next to him, my legs hanging off. He leaned in for another kiss; this time he gave me two short pecks on the lips. I was a little scared, but we just lay there. We stared at each other until Kaisen broke the silence.

"I have liked you since we first met." He said as he brushed a piece of my hair behind my ear. "And after talking to you on the phone, I like you even more, Charlotte."

"I liked you right away, too." I told him. "I like you a lot." He smiled at me and leaned down to kiss me. There was a quick knock on the door. We both jumped to our feet and heard Harper from behind the door.

"Good night, guys." We both laughed in relief.

"You should probably try to get some sleep, it's late." Kaisen says to me.

Kaisen walked me to his door. He leaned down to give me a peck on the lips before he opened the door. "Good night." I said.

"Sweet dreams." He replied as I walked down the hall to my room.

The storm was still raging when I finally fell asleep sometime between three and four in the morning. My dreams weren't pleasant.

I was standing in a wet, dark hay field, facing a large stone building that looked like a cage. The ground was too soft and mushy from all of the rain. The storm was fierce, blowing the grass and trees from their roots. I could barely keep my balance from the strength of the nature around me. The lighting struck the ground a few hundred feet from where I was standing. The flash of light so close scared me, knocking me to the ground. Another flash of lighting, this time it struck the large mysterious cage, gouging a large stone piece from the left corner, leaving a gaping hole. Smoke came from the opening and I could hear screams coming from inside the building. I watched in horror as a shadowy figure emerged from the large opening created by the lightning. A large crash of thunder shook my whole body, still lying in the long hay. The rain was pelting me in the face so hard I could barely see as the bleak outline of a person glided quickly towards me. I was frozen in my spot, unable to even make a sound. As the shape got closer I could see it was a bald man, with dark eyebrows. He looked down at me as he was only feet away now. He petrified me, I didn't know who he was but he didn't look friendly. As he bent down towards me, I could see he was wearing very worn and tattered clothing under his cloak. His eyes were fierce and as green as my ring, which was now glowing on my finger the, same glow as his eyes. In a startling deep voice he said "You must be Charlotte?"

I woke up with beads of sweat on my forehead. I threw off my blankets and sat up thinking about who I saw in my nightmare. It was someone I had never seen before, and I was glad I didn't know him. He was terrifying and definitely wasn't asking my name in a friendly way. Maybe it was nothing more than my imagination getting to me. I looked at the clock, 9:45. I wonder why no one came to wake me for breakfast. I climbed out of bed taking off my ring and leaving it on my nightstand as I headed downstairs.

"…you found him yet?" David was talking on the phone as I entered the dining room. "Good morning Charlotte." He said as he left the room to talk privately.

"Good morning." I said. "Where are the boys?" I asked noticing that Marilyn was the only other one at breakfast.

"They are still sleeping. Chef Mallow said you kids couldn't sleep because of the storm so I let you sleep later than usual." Marilyn explained. "Did you get any sleep last night?"

"I slept but had a terrible dream." I told her with a yawn.

"I bet the storm didn't help it any. What was the dream about?"

"I was staring up into the storm and then lightning struck a dark brick building and I could feel the rumble of the building breaking so well it was like the storm shook my whole room." I explained to her.

Marilyn seemed really interested in my dream and she had me explain the whole thing, including the creepy guy who knew who I was. When I told her about the broken building her eyes widened, but she tried to keep her composure until after my story was over. She seemed fascinated by the details and asked questions about the stranger. She asked what he looked like and gave specifics to his features, like she knew exactly who I was talking about. Once she had finished her questions she took me to David and had me explain my dream to him as well.

My dream was about Balano-Regelnin King, he has escaped from Zweb, and no one can find him. They weren't sure how I dreamt this or how detailed I was able to see it happen, but I was reassured that I was in no harm and I didn't have anything to worry about, which only made me begin to worry. David was sure I was in no danger but just to be safe I was allowed to leave for America to visit Luke and Louis two days early. The precaution wasn't necessary after all. Bala King could not be found and no one reported seeing him which meant he wasn't coming after me like I saw in my dream. There was speculation that he is going to stay in hiding until he can regain his strength. When someone goes to Zweb they are given a meal that keeps them alive but weak and they are in a room that restricts their powers so they can't harm anyone. Once a week they are taken to a room where the guards surround them and dual with their powers. They do this so the prisoners stay weak, the more they battle the more tired and warn out they will become, especially when they aren't doing up keep with their powers. If they were practicing daily their powers wouldn't suffer as much.

Chapter 10

KAISEN AND HARPER TOOK me to the airport while Dad and Marilyn had to have a meeting with the other rulers of Andeka. “I can't believe you actually had a dream about Bala breaking out of Zweb. How did you do that?” Harper asked when we got into the car.

“I am not sure, it wasn't like any other dream I have ever had before. It was as if it was real and I was actually there. It freaked me out.” I told them. Kaisen held my hand as he drove. I felt so much safer when we were touching.

“I bet it did. He is pretty scary.” Harper said.

“Harper, you don't know that, you don't even remember him.” Kaisen said a little on edge.

“You have met him?” I asked.

“Well yeah we have met him, he...” Kaisen cut off Harper mid-sentence.

“He tried to kill us, okay, can we not talk about this anymore. Please.” Kaisen said as he squeezed my hand lightly.

The boys didn't say anything else; they exchanged a warning glance then changed the subject.

"So, Charlie, how long are you staying with your step-dad?" Harper asked.

"A week, I will be back the day after Christmas." I answered.

"That sucks, that is such a long time to be gone. You will get back just in time to go to the Winter Palace, though. You will love it." Harper said.

"It will be a long time but I miss my brother so much, I haven't seen him since May. I can't wait to see him."

"He is five right?" Kaisen asked, remembering from one of our phone conversations.

"Yeah, March will be his first birthday I don't spend with him, so we are celebrating it while I am there." I say as Kaisen squeezes my hand again.

We pulled up to the pick-up and drop off area of the airport. Both Kaisen and Harper got out of the car. Kaisen pulled my suitcase from the trunk while Harper said goodbye to me.

"Well, have fun on your trip. Don't tell anyone about your powers, but keep practicing." Harper started. He hugged me.

"I will." I told him as he released his grip and climbed into the front seat of the car. Kaisen looked at me a little funny when he pulled my luggage up to the curb.

He stopped a foot away from me. "Do you have your ticket?" I just nodded. "Okay, have a good Christmas with your family. I'll see you in a week." He smiled at me but didn't make a move towards me. From all of the conversations on the phone,

I feel like I have known him forever. I can already tell when something is bothering him. I stepped towards him and took his hand in mine.

“I'm sorry if we upset you earlier, I didn't know about...” I said trailing off, hoping he knew what I was talking about.

“No, Harper is what upset me, he talks too much and since he doesn't remember it, he just tells the story how he heard it and... It's fine.” We stood there for a few seconds of silence just looking at each other.

“I'll miss you.” I said. “May I call you while I'm gone?” He smiles at me and leans down and gently presses his lips to mine. My stomach flutters as he pulls me to him. I almost forget that there are other people around us.

“I'll miss you too. And you can call me whenever you want.” Kaisen said as he lets go of me but holds tight to my hand. “I'll see you in one week.”

“Bye” I said as I drop his hand and put my hand around the handle of my suitcase.

“Bye, Charlie.” My stomach fluttered when he said my nickname. I smiled at him while I walked into the airport towards the security check-point. He had never called me Charlie before. Everyone else calls me that now, but I especially like it when he says it.

Chapter 11

MY WEEK WITH Luke and Louis went by fast and at the end, I wish I had more time with them. It was hard at first, though. We took flowers to my mother's grave and I spent time with my grandparents and Luke's family. I went to dinner with my friend Holly, who I hadn't talked to since I left. We talked for hours about Kaisen and Harper and I told her about the beautiful house and the maids and chef. I told her everything that was going on with my new life, well everything except Andeka. We celebrated Louis' birthday and, of course, Christmas. I even went to Louis' Christmas Concert at his school. He was one of the sheep. He showed me his toys and his games that he liked to play. I had a lot of fun and I had missed being here with them, but I knew I had to go back. Late at night when everyone had gone to bed I would call Kaisen, but every time I called him he didn't answer. I needed to not think about Kaisen so much when I was on vacation with Luke and Louis. I would have plenty of time to talk to Kaisen. And maybe that is why he wasn't answering his phone. I tried not to let it bother me.

Luke and Louis,

Even though I just got back to Europe, I miss you already. I had fun visiting you and hope I get to see you again soon. Thank you again for the new camera for Christmas. I will be sure to take plenty of pictures to send you both. I won't be able to email while on vacation but I will let you know when I get back. I love you.

Charlotte

Dad picked me up at the airport at two o'clock the day after Christmas. Even though I knew it was going to be a long time before I would see Louis again I had to admit I missed David's home. I was ready to go back, the memories of my past hurt too much to really enjoy myself and I wanted to get back to spend time with Kaisen before he had to go back to school. I was pretty sure I was in love with him, but I didn't really know how much he actually liked me and I was a scared to ask, especially since he wasn't answering my calls.

Marilyn had taken the boys shopping with her this morning and they weren't back yet. I repacked my suitcase for the winter lodge while I waited for everyone to get home. After finishing my bags, I showered and changed. While I was drying my hair in my room I heard a knock at my door. When I opened it Harper walked half asleep into me and hugged me, which was sort of strange. “It's been boring here without you.” He whispered into my ear like it was a secret. “I think I'm still sleeping.” I laughed.

“What is wrong with you?” I joked with Harper.

“I have only slept three hours, maybe less and I fell asleep on the way back here from shopping and I feel really funny, like I’m drunk, only except I’m not, at least I don't think I am. I don't know, I didn't drink anything.” He said releasing me and stepping back. His eyes drooping and his head tilted back so he could see through the crack between his eye lids.

“Why were you up so late?” I asked him.

“I don't remember, Kaisen wouldn't let me go to sleep, something about taking him to a red stream. I don't know, maybe I was hallucinating, because now that I say that, it doesn’t make sense.” He said with a yawn. His babbling was amusing but I sent him off to his room to get more sleep.

I went down stairs to see Marilyn and Kaisen once Harper was gone. Marilyn was talking with Dad about the plans for the next few weeks at the Winter Lodge. I guess its somewhere in Andeka, where Cigam Rulers go on vacation. Marilyn is worried that Bala King will show up there because he knows that the rulers will be there this time of year. Dad thinks she is just paranoid. When Bala escaped from Zweb the last two times, he tried to assassinate the rulers of Andeka, starting with Marilyn and the boys. She is afraid he will try that again. Dad thinks that it would be better to get away from the home for a while in case he shows up here. I never thought that Andeka would be so dangerous.

“Merry Christmas, Charlie.” Marilyn says as she sees me come down the stairs.

"Merry Christmas." She hugged me. "Did you see Harper and Kaisen? They went up to say hi and then go to sleep. Harper was acting strange. I guess they both stayed up late last night getting Christmas Presents for everyone. They will probably sleep the rest of the day if I let them."

"I did see Harper, he was babbling about sleeping three hours and that he wanted more sleep." I laughed.

"Well, I think they can sleep two more hours, and then I will wake them so we can celebrate Christmas with dinner and presents." She smiled.

"You guys didn't need to wait for me." I told her.

"It's your first Christmas here with us, of course we needed to wait. You are a part of this family too, Charlotte." She said.

"Thank you." I told her.

ABOUT AN HOUR later Harper came back to my room. "Hey... what did I say to you earlier?" He asked.

"Nothing really, just glad that I'm home and that you only got three hours of sleep because Kaisen needed to take you to the red river." I told him with a laugh. "What did you guys do last night?" I asked.

"I guess we went to a red stream." He said as he laughed. "Just making sure I didn't say anything stupid, which I did." He smiled. "I am glad that you are back though, it was boring here without you, I'm not sure what Kaisen and I did before you moved in." He laughed. After he left my room, I debated whether it was alright to go wake up Kaisen. Marilyn did say two hours and it had only been one, but I really wanted to see him. I wonder why he didn't come say hi to me before he took a nap.

I decided not to wake up Kaisen and went downstairs to talk to Marilyn instead. She was wrapping presents and let me help. Mine were already wrapped but today she bought Dad's gift.

"I always wait as long as I can to get gifts. The day after Christmas always has really good sales." She told me.

After wrapping presents I went upstairs to gather up the presents I bought for everyone. I got an extra present for Kaisen but still wasn't sure if I was going to give it to him yet or not. I still hadn't seen him yet since I had been back today, he didn't answer any of my calls while I was gone and he didn't say hi to me before he went to sleep. Maybe I'm over thinking this. He told me that he really liked me before I left. I will just wait and see what he says when I see him. I told myself. As I walked out of my room with an arm full of gifts, Kaisen walked out of his room with a few gifts of his own.

"Hi," I said to him. He smiled at me with his intoxicating grin.

"Hi," he said as he walked beside me down to the tree where we dropped off our gifts and started to head back to our rooms. "How was your trip to Iowa?"

"I really enjoyed it. My brother has grown a lot since I saw him last." I told him.

"I bet he really missed you. I..." He started.

"Kaisen," Marilyn interrupted us, but I don't think she noticed. "I'm glad you are awake, it's almost time for dinner, and will you get Harper?"

"Sure, Mom." He said as we turned to go upstairs.

"Charlotte, will you come here for a minute?" She asked me as she took me to her office. "I bought you a winter coat and boots for the trip and forgot to ask you earlier to try them on to make sure they fit." She said as she laid out a beautiful beige coat with fur collar and matching beige boots. There was also a white hat and gloves.

"Thank you," I said as I tried everything on. And like always, everything fit perfect.

Once I came out of Marilyn's office I planned to see Kaisen, but dinner was ready and the boys were downstairs waiting for everyone else.

We had a few Andekan delicacies including oven baked snogcumple, a southern Andekan bird, Dhesin eggs, a form of frog caviar and harlinrod dessert, a sweet flavored yellow flower. I didn't care for the Dhesin eggs but everything else tasted good. After we ate dinner we opened presents. I got Marilyn and Dad a bag of coffee beans from Guatemala and a set of coffee mugs. I didn't have a lot of money to spend on them and I knew that they like coffee. They gave me money to spend on the boys but told me not to spend it on them. I had a hard time shopping for the boys. What do I get two teenagers that have everything that they need and want? They are spoiled but are humble. They don't need that stuff but Marilyn likes giving them gifts for doing well in school. I got Harper an air soft rifle with a small revolver and Kaisen two air soft hand pistols. I bought masks, a large container of ammo and extra magazines for each of their guns. The boys have never had weapons before, but dad told me it was alright to have these.

They hurt much less than paintball guns and it was something that I used to do back at home with my friends over the summer. Once they opened my presents I opened their presents. Kaisen got me a tablet and Harper got me gift cards for the tablet. Marilyn and Dad bought me a six-speed Scion Tc Series 8.0. They also got me an air soft sniper rifle and extra gear to go with it. Then, of course, the boys and I got the usual things parents give for Christmas: Socks, School Clothes, Shoes, and gift cards to some of our favorite stores.

After opening presents and talking with each other, I took my presents to my room. We were planning to leave early in the morning for the winter lodge so we all needed to go to bed soon. Marilyn went to finish packing and Dad went to his office to finish up some work. I put on my pajamas and crawled in bed with my new tablet. I had just set up my account and opened up my email when Kaisen knocked on my door. He had a small present in his hand.

"May I come in?" He asked with a smile. I smiled back at him and let him into my room.

"What's up?" I asked him, trying to act natural.

"The ceiling." He said, looking up, and then smiling big as he looked back at me. I blushed a little. "I have something for you, but I couldn't give it to you downstairs." He put his fingers under my chin and pulled my face up to his. My stomach fluttered as he kissed my lips lightly. He tried to make it a quick kiss but as he parted our lips I pushed up onto my toes and reconnected them. I put my arms around his neck and pulled him to me. He wrapped his arms around me and stood up, lifting me off the ground. When he put me back down I let go of his neck, letting my hands fall to his biceps.

"I missed you too." I said. Kaisen gently released me and held out the box for me. "Merry Christmas." He said.

"What is this? You already gave me my gift." I told him.

"I wanted to get you two gifts." He told me with a grin. His smiles are so intoxicating; they always make me smile back. I got out his other present I bought him and held it out for him. He tilted his head slightly to one side and gave me a hypocritical glare.

"What is this? You already gave me my gift." He copied. I blushed as he took the box from my hand.

"You first." He said, sitting down on the couch. I opened the present and inside was a silver charm bracelet with a single silver open heart charm.

"It's beautiful, thank you." I said as I took the bracelet out of the box. Kaisen latched it around my wrist for me then leaned over for a quick kiss. When he opened the gift I got him he laughed.

"Now we match." He said as he pulled out a thin gold chained bracelet. This gift is why I had to ask Marilyn and Dad for money for the other gifts.

"I wasn't sure if you wore jewelry or not." I told him, hoping he liked it. He smiled and pulled his long sleeve up over his wrist and showed me a silver bracelet.

"Now I have silver and gold." He said. "Thank you, I really like it." He had me take off his silver bracelet and put on the gold one. He smiled at me and pulled me in for another kiss, this time was longer. My stomach started to flutter like I was going over the first big drop on a roller coaster. My eyes closed and my heart accelerated as our lips moved together in sync. The gift box and wrapping paper fell from my lap as I leaned forward into him. He pulled me onto his lap as he leaned back on the coach more, being careful not to break our lip lock. My face got hot as my nerves jumped. His breathing picked up as his lips parted and his tongue followed my lips to my tongue. I wanted to keep going but my lungs were screaming for air so I broke the kiss off as he laughed under his breath.

"I like you a lot Charlotte." He said gazing into my eyes.

I couldn't help but smile and bite down on my lower lip. "I like you a lot, too."

He smiled back and pulled me down for more kisses. I was laying on him now as he lay out on the couch. He pulled me in tighter with every kiss. I wanted this night to never end. We had to be up early in the morning so after a few minutes Kaisen broke our lip lock. He kissed me on the forehead before he returned to his room. Holy crap, that was hot!

Chapter 12

MARILYN WOKE ME up early the next morning. Normally we ride in the limo anytime we go anywhere as a family, but this trip dad drove us in the Hummer. We needed extra room to take all the bags and the snow gear. I sat between Kaisen and Harper in the back seat. It was a five hour drive to the Winter Lodge. We slept most of the way there and when I woke up Kaisen and Harper were awake. Marilyn showed me a picture on her phone. It was the three of us sleeping. Kaisen was lying on the door with his arm around me. My head was on his shoulder and Harper's head was on my side with my arm around Harper. Marilyn thought it was the sweetest thing she had ever seen.

The employees at the lodge we stayed at unpacked the car while Kaisen, Harper and I got our snow gear on and went out to the ski lift. I rode with Kaisen and Harper rode alone.

“Wow,” I said looking out at the view as we climbed to the top of the snow hill. “It’s so beautiful up here.”

"You're supposed to tell her she makes it more beautiful." Harper shouted at us from the seat behind us. I laughed. Kaisen shook his head as he laughed.

"Charlotte, it has never been more beautiful up here until right at this moment, because I'm up here with you." Kaisen said.

"Now, kiss her." Harper shouted at Kaisen.

"Harper! Shut up!" Kaisen shouted back at him. He turned back around and looked at me.

"You should just kiss me so you will make him leave you alone." I joked.

"I'm sure that's the only reason you want me to kiss you." He laughed as he leaned in and kissed me. "You really are beautiful." He said between three small pecks on the lips.

"Thank you." I said as we got to the top of the hill.

"Have you ever snowboarded before?" Kaisen asked me when we got to the part of the hill where we would be going down.

"A few times." I lied. I have snowboarded every winter since I was twelve. My mom would ski while I would snowboard with Luke.

"I will go down first and make a path for you, if you want." He said.

"No way, I want to race." I told him.

"Sweet," Harper said. "What are the stakes?"

"Charlotte, are you sure? I don't want you to get hurt if you don't know what you are doing." Kaisen said.

"I have done this before, don't worry. I will be fine." I told Kaisen, then I turned to Harper. "How about if I win you can't mention anything about Kaisen and I the whole time we are here."

"And if I win?" Harper asked with a grin.

"Charlotte, we come here every year. Harper is really good at snowboarding." Kaisen said. "Don't let him win anything you will regret."

"If you win I will be your servant the whole time we are here."

"Charlotte!" Kaisen exclaimed shaking his head.

"Do you want to be in this bet?" I asked.

"Yeah, if I win Harper can't mention anything about us the whole time. If you win I will wait on you and give you whatever you want the whole trip." He said to me.

"Okay, do we all have a deal? No powers, no tripping each other and no cheating." I said. "We all start at the same time."

"Okay," Harper said with a smile. "I really hope you know what you are doing Charlotte."

"How hard can it be?" I asked. Harper and Kaisen both gave me wide eyed glance.

"Serious? Have you ever done this?" Kaisen asked.

"I'll be fine. Ready? Get set...go." I said as I jumped up and over the hillside. I didn't look back as I increased speed down the hill. As I neared the bottom of the hill I saw a ramp a few yards away. I guided my board behind the ramp and heard Harper and Kaisen both scream at me. I glanced back at them as I went up the ramp. They were coming up behind me, but still far enough behind so that I could win this race and show off a bit. I grabbed the bottom of my board and brought it above my head then release my hand as I let my feet guide it back down to the ground and landed the jump almost perfect. I stopped at the bottom of the hill and waiting for Kaisen and Harper to get down there.

"What the hell was that?" Harper asked as they both came to a stop.

"I told you that I have done with before." I smirked.

"You cheated. You didn't tell us that you were really good." Harper complained.

Kaisen started to laugh. "She won fair and square; you can't say anything to either of us about our relationship at all. Good job baby, can I carry your board over to the lift?" Kaisen smiled.

"Yes you can." I smiled. "Harper you should know that if I challenge you to something, it means that I'm going to win."

"Best two out of three?" Harper asks.

"Nah, I already won, why would I want to chance losing, I already have my servant." I joked as I pecked Kaisen on the cheek and walked away.

"Damn, she was really good." I heard Harper tell Kaisen.

"DID YOU HAVE fun today?" Dad asked me while we sat together on the large couch in front of a fireplace. The winter palace was almost like a log cabin, everything was wood and winter colors. I could definitely tell it was Christmas time. Everything was warm and cozy.

"Yeah, my butt hurts from falling down all week, but I've had a lot of fun." I smiled at him as I took a sip of my hot apple cinnamon cider. Harper and Kaisen have been teaching me new jumps off the ramps. Tonight, when we got back to the lodge

Marilyn and Dad were waiting for us outside. They started a snowball fight.

I told Dad about beating Kaisen and Harper at a race the first day we were here and told him that Kaisen was my personal servant and Harper wasn't allowed to make fun of me the whole time we are here. I didn't tell him the part about Kaisen and me for obvious reasons. He thought it was funny that I beat them AND got them to agree to ridiculous terms.

“Hey Charlotte. When you’re free, you should come up and hang out with Kaisen and me.” Harper said with a laugh as he passed through the living room.

“Alright, I’ll be up in a bit.” I called after him.

“Go ahead. I am going to see if Marilyn needs help cooking dinner. I’ll come get you guys when it’s ready.” Dad said kissing my forehead then left the room.

I climbed the stairs to the pool hall. Harper was playing video games on the big screen television. “Kaisen wants you in his room.” He said pointing to the large double doors behind him.

“We aren't all going to hang out?” I asked. Harper shrugged.

I knocked on the large double doors, but before I could lie my knuckles on the wood for a second time the door cracked open and Kaisen grabbed my hand and pulled me in. He placed one hand on the small of my back and pulled me close. Before I could say anything, his lips were pressed against mine. I instantly felt like I was melting in his arms. His body was so warm and his lips were gentle and his touch was soft and loving. I couldn’t get enough of this wonderful feeling. I never wanted it to stop and for him to initiate it just made it that much better.

"Your heart is pounding." Kaisen said, breaking off our kiss. "Are you okay?"

"I'm great," I said, lifting myself up to try and reconnect our lips. He smiled at me and bent down a little so I could reach, but then he picked me up, cradling me in his arms and pulling me close. Our lips reconnected as he walked through his room with me. I knew exactly where he was taking me and no matter how much I cared about him, his bed was the last place I wanted his mind to be. He placed me gently down on the middle of his king size bed, without our lips leaving each other's. He crawled over me onto the bed. My heart was really racing now, I started to get really warm and I couldn't breathe. I wanted him to slow down, I didn't like being on his bed, I wasn't sure what he was thinking, but it was making me uncomfortable wondering what was going on in his mind.

"What's wrong?" He asked with a worried look on his face.

"Nothing, why?"

"You're… uh, I don't know how to explain it. You are using your powers," He said.

"No I'm not." I said confused.

"Yes, you are. I can barely kiss you. It seems like an invisible hand is pushing me back. I didn't know you knew how to do that." He explained.

"I didn't know I was doing it. I'm sorry." I said. Kaisen sat up on the bed and I followed, leaning against the large headboard next to him. I still wasn't sure how a Shaire's powers worked but I was making them happen without even knowing it.

"Charlotte, do you like me?" Kaisen asked with another worried look on his face.

"What? Of course I do." I said, stunned.

"Are you sure? Why don't you want me to kiss you then? Am I bad kisser?"

"No, I like kissing you." I wasn't sure what he was worried about.

"Well, why are you trying to get me to stop? If you wanted to kiss me, I wouldn't feel you trying to stop me." He explained.

"I don't even know how to do that." I tried to tell him.

"What were you just thinking about?" I wasn't sure how to answer that. "Are we moving too fast?" I did want to kiss him, but that is all I wanted to do at this point. His bed just makes me nervous because he is older than me and I'm not sure how experienced.

"I don't know." I lied at first then I took a deep breath, I had to tell him eventually, or I might do something I will regret. "I was thinking about where we are. I do want to kiss you; I just don't want to kiss you here."

"Why? We kiss at home. Is it because Harper is in the other room, because he won't say anything?"

"No. It's… well… your bed." I hid my face from him when I said this, unsure of his reaction. He laughed.

"Oh, Charlotte, I didn't mean to make you uncomfortable." He started as he brought my face up to look into his eyes. "I swear, sex never crossed my mind."

"Okay," I said. He kissed my lips again.

"I brought you up here to give you something." He said as he reached over to his bedside table and pulled something out of the top drawer. "I wanted to give this to you for Christmas but it wasn't finished." He placed a red charm in my hand.

"You made this?" I asked.

"I had the crystal but I had to alter it so it was small enough for a charm on your bracelet and I added the clasp."

"Thank you, it's beautiful." I leaned over and gave him a peck on the cheek. "Will you put it on my bracelet?"

"Is that an official request?" He joked, referring to our deal. He didn't wait for an answer and placed the charm next to my first charm. "I still can't believe that you beat us."

"I have been snowboarding since I was real young. My mom used to take me every winter to a ski lodge with her family." I said, remembering the fun times I used to have with my mom. "We would race, she would ski, and I would snowboard. And who ever won would buy hot cocoa at a coffee shop at the bottom of one of the hills next to the rental place." Thinking about my mom and how much fun we had made my eyes start to water. Kaisen wiped away a tear that was rolling down my face. I haven't cried in a long time. It was weird to all of a sudden have that intense empty feeling in my chest when I was thinking of my mother. I felt it after she died but it started to not hurt as bad when I started spending time with Marilyn and Dad. Then when I met Harper and Kaisen it completely disappeared. I didn't replace her with them; I just had people to get my mind off of it.

"Charlotte, are you alright?" Kaisen asked. I didn't even realize that I was staring down at my hands as tears rolled down my face.

"Yeah, I'm fine." I told him as I wiped the tears from my face. He leaned over and grabbed a tissue off the bedside table and handed it to me. "I'm sorry."

"Don't apologize. It's alright to cry, Charlie." He told me.

"I know, I just don't like to cry in front of people." I said as I wiped away the last of the tears in my eyes and took a deep breath so I could clear my mind and steady my emotions.

"Charlie, you aren't around people, you are with me. And crying doesn't make you any less tough." He said. I knew he was right, but I still didn't want to cry in front of him.

"I know." I said. "Can we change the subject, please?"

"Yeah, what do you want to talk about?"

"Anything else." I told him. He pulled my face to his and looked into my eyes for a few seconds before he kissed me. My stomach fluttered like it usually does when he kissed me. We made out for a few minutes, and then he pulled away.

"Oh, I forgot to tell you. I know that Harper knows about us, but we can't tell our friends. Connor and Jessie Darby are heirs to a kingdom here and there is an ambassador here with their two children. You danced with their son at the banquet, Lex, and he has a sister, Luica. They are all going to be here this week while we are here and we will probably see them tomorrow. They can't know about us."

"I understand. I won't tell anyone. Do you think Harper will say anything?"

"No, but I'm going to talk to him to make sure." Kaisen takes my hand in his. "Charlotte, there is something I need to tell you. I..." He is cut off by a knock at the door.

"Kaisen, can I come in?" David asks from the other side of the door. We both freeze and my cheeks get warm. Oh shit. We are definitely busted. Kaisen motions for me to hide in the bathroom; I get up from the bed and start for the bathroom. I don't even get half way there when my dad opens the bedroom door. I freeze where I am and take in a deep breath. As I close my eyes I feel hands wrap around my body and when I open my eyes back up I'm standing in my room with Harper.

"You are so damn lucky that I was paying attention." Harper said. He dropped his hands and I through my arms around him.

"Thank you so much. I can't believe that you did that. Holy crap, I can't believe that happened." I freaked out. I let go of him. "I owe you big." I told him.

"I know. I will think of something that you can do to repay me." He joked.

"Oh, Kaisen was going to talk to you, tomorrow we are seeing our friends. Please don't tell anyone about Kaisen and me."

"I won't tell anyone. I promise." He told me. "But I can't promise they won't find out, especially if they see you and Kaisen look at each other."

"What?"

"You can tell something is up between the two of you just by looking at you guys. You will have to work real hard even when you are around our parents. It is starting to get obvious that you like each other."

"Okay, thank you, I will try."

"Well, it's time for dinner, which is what David came to tell Kaisen. I told him that I would tell you so he wouldn't come up here."

THE COLD WIND BIT my nose and cheeks as I walked out the back patio door of the palace, into the beautiful winter morning. This morning all of the trees were covered in new fallen snow and more was falling in large clumps that resembled cotton. The Darby's had arrived last night to their palace down the street. Jessie and Connor planned to meet us at the top of one of the hills for tubing. The tubes were as wide as I was tall. They looked heavy too, good thing there was a tube/sled lift, so we could be lazy, we didn't have to walk up the hill or carry up a tube, and we just let the lifts do those jobs for us.

"Charlotte, you remember Lex and Luica Trechner?" Jessie asked me then turned to the others, "I figured it would be more fun with more people." Lex smiled at me and I smiled back to be polite.

"So, what hill do you want to start on?" Connor asked.

"Let's start small and work our way up. But let's skip the bunny trail; that is too boring. The back side of the ski slope has more steep inclines that are better for sleds and tubes." Kaisen suggested.

I avoided Lex as best I could for the first hour of tubing. I tried to stay close to Jessie, racing her down the hills, but Lex kept trying to get closer.

"Charlotte, you should come with me on my tube. We can race Luica and Kaisen." He suggested. Why would I want to do that… oh yeah, no one knows about Kaisen and I, except Harper. Ugh, I didn't like this. I was more jealous than I thought I would be and it was getting in the way of acting as if I didn't like Kaisen.

"Yeah, that sounds like fun, team races." Luica agreed. Kaisen didn't argue with them, he smiled at me and got on the tube with Luica, which I guess meant he wasn't jealous that Lex was hitting on me. I was glad though, that was the only reason I was avoiding him. I didn't want a fight to break out or anything, I wasn't sure if Kaisen was the jealous type and I wasn't willing to find out the hard way.

"On your marks, get set, GO!" Jessie said as Connor pushed Lex and I, and Harper pushed Kaisen and Luica over the hill. Our tubes traveled fast down the steep incline, and I could see Kaisen and Luica gently pulling ahead of us. We started to slow a bit and I could see Kaisen and Luica in head of us now, nearing the finish line.

"Hold on tight." Lex told me as he grabbed on to me around my waist with one hand and the tube with the other. Before I could protest my eyes started to blur and we started accelerating, then my eyes focused back in again and we were at the bottom of the hill stopped. I turned to look back up the hill and saw that Kaisen and Luica were just pulling in next to us.

"You cheated." Luica yelled.

"So did you." Lex reproached.

"How did we cheat, you transported to the finish line so you could win."

"Don't be a sore loser, sis. Come on Charlotte, let's go again." Lex said as he put the tube onto the lift and motioned me to get on the ski lift with him. I looked at Kaisen as I walked away, he was smiling and he winked at me, so I knew he wouldn't be mad if I played along and made Lex happy.

"How do you like it here?" Lex asked when we were alone on the lift.

"It's cold but I'm enjoying it, and it's beautiful."

"It's more beautiful when you're here." He said. It reminded me of the first time I was up here with Kaisen.

"Thanks." I said.

"I mean it, you are very pretty." He said putting his hand on mine. I picked up his hand and set it on top of his lap and put my hands in my own lap, trying not to be too mean. "What's wrong? Can't I hold your hand; you just said its cold out."

"I don't like to be touched, that's all."

"So, I guess that means no to a kiss?"

"It does. I'm sorry, Lex, I just don't see you like that."

"Do you have a boyfriend?" He asked.

"No, I…"

"But you have a crush on someone?" I didn't say anything, I just looked at him.

"Well, who is it?" He pried.

What am I supposed to say? I am not a good liar; I can't say a good lie, let alone make one up on the spot that would be believable.

"Is it someone from school?" He asked.

"Yes."

"Well does he like you back?"

"I don't know."

"Well, he must be a lucky guy for you to like him." He said as we reached the top of the slopes, thank goodness. "Well, I like you Charlotte; you are smart and so beautiful. Maybe you should crush on someone who likes you back." He winked at me as he walked away. I waited a few more seconds for Kaisen and Luica to get to the top. Luica was leaning on Kaisen's shoulder, which made me jealous but I could handle it, I hoped.

"Are you girls having fun?" Kaisen asked us both.

"Yeah, this is great. We should get together more often." Luica started. "Charlotte, you and Lex look like you're having fun together."

"Yeah, I guess. I wasn't ready for him to transport me to the bottom of the hill though, it scared me." I tried joking with them.

Tubing for the rest of the time was boring, Luica hung around Kaisen mostly and I tried avoiding Lex as much as I could. I made Harper my official racing team mate. I wouldn't let him out of my sight, pretty much.

When we got back to the palace for lunch around two, I was starving, tired and wet from sitting in the snow. I ate lunch, took a hot bath and snuggled up on the couch in the game room with a book and a blanket. It didn't take long for Kaisen to find me; I hadn't even read one chapter.

"How was your day today?" Kaisen asked as he sat down beside me under the blankets. He pulled me towards him, leaning me up against him. I put my book down and rested my head against his chest. He was so warm and I loved when his arms were around me. It made me feel so safe. I could sit here with him forever.

"Fine, how was yours?"

"Eh, it could have gone better." He said. He seemed tense, more than he did earlier when we were tubing with Lex and Luica.

"It wasn't that bad, was it?"

"No, it just sucked pretending to flirt with someone else and not get jealous you were spending time with someone else."

"I know what you mean." I told him. "Oh, there was something you wanted to tell me the other night. What was it?"

"There IS something that I need to tell you. You aren't going to like it at all." I waited for him to tell me whatever it was that was bothering him. "Just please don't be mad at me."

"Kaisen, what are you talking about?" I asked. Kaisen's pleading voice frightened me. I couldn't help but think the worst. Was he going to break up with me? Wait. Are we technically dating? What are we to each other? Boyfriend/ Girlfriend?

"Just please promise me you won't be mad. I wanted to tell you before now but I didn't know how and I care about you so much."

"Kaisen, hon, what's wrong? You're scaring me, just tell me."

"Promise me first, I won't tell you unless I know you won't get mad, I don't think I can handle this if you're mad at me."

"Okay, I promise. Now, please, tell me." My hands had started to squeeze my book, causing my knuckles to turn a pale white color. I put the book on the table next to the couch so I wouldn't end up wrecking it.

Kaisen took a deep breath, took my hands in his and said, "When I was young, times in Andeka were real bad. I mean, there were death threats on my mother constantly. Harper and I weren't very safe either. When my mother was pregnant with Harper, someone broke into our house and killed my grandparents. Then they came after my mom and I. After that my mom arranged a marriage for me so if something happened to her Harper and I would go live with the family of the girl I will marry. They would raise us. Then we would get married and take over my mother's throne. " It took me a few seconds to comprehend what he was saying.

"You're engaged." I tried to hold back any anger he might hear. I removed my hands from his. I wasn't sure what else to say. What did this mean? How long would it be until he gets married? Why wasn't I allowed to get mad at him for this?

"If you say it like that then I've been engaged since I was three. But I barely see her and I don't like her."

"You are getting married?" I asked as a lump rose in my throat. I could barely speak so I whispered. "When?"

"Not for a while. She is two years younger than me. I plan to finish college first. I have been trying to push it off as long as

I can. Her parents want us to date for a while before the wedding."

"But you're getting married." My voice was so quiet, now. I was trying not to be angry with him. I understand that he didn't have a say in the matter but I like him so much, I feel like he was leading me on, because he knew that we could never have a real relationship. I don't mean that I love him enough to marry him, but for him to date me to pass time is appalling.

"Charlotte, please, I didn't mean to upset you. I just wanted to tell you the truth. I haven't dated anyone in a long time because this reason."

"Then why did you kiss me? Why did you tell me you liked me?"

"Because, I do like you. Charlotte, I like you so much. I didn't mean to hurt you. I just needed you to know before you find out from someone else." He said trying to take me hand again. I slowly pulled it away.

"To who?" My voice broke. I hadn't even thought of this before now. Have I met his fiancé? Was I friends with her? I don't know if I could stand to watch Kaisen get married to anyone, especially one of my friends.

"Charlotte, honey, don't be upset. I'm sorry; I don't have any control over this. I would undo it if I could." He tried to take my hand a third time. She was someone I knew. Why wouldn't he tell me who it was if I didn't know her? I could feel tears well up in the corner of my eyes; I tried to keep them from spilling over my eyelids. I really don't want to cry in front of him again.

"Is it anyone I know?" Kaisen paused for a few short seconds. Why wouldn't he just tell me? Was it that bad? I couldn't stand it anymore; I needed to know who it was. "Kaisen, who?" I said, almost screaming now.

"Luica." I think a part of me already knew who it was before I asked. I don't think I can look at her the same. I know it's not her fault but I can't help but hate her or envy her or something. "Charlotte, I don't want you mad at me, which is why I told you now, instead of later." He tried to kiss my hands but I pulled them away and up to my face to hide behind them. I wanted to scream. My eyes couldn't hold anything back anymore. Tears came streaming down my face behind my hands. I leaned over and put my face into my lap. "Charlotte, please, look at me."

"I can't." I said through my hands.

"Hon, please."

"Will you please just go?"

"Charlotte, please?" He started. But I didn't want to hear it, I wanted to be alone, so I got up and left the room. I didn't want him to see me cry, I didn't usually cry. I listen to see if he was following me but he wasn't. I sat up in my room and cried for a while. Then after I stopped I thought about what just happened.

What did it matter if he was going to get married to someone else, did I really believe he cared enough about me to want to be with me long enough to consider marriage? We haven't been dating long, if we are even actually dating at all. Could I ever marry Kaisen? I wasn't sure. I wasn't sure how I could ever tell Dad that I was sort of dating Kaisen behind his back. Maybe this is for the best. More tears came down my cheeks at the thought of not being with him though. My stomach turned over and I felt sick. I like Kaisen so much. What was I saying…? I love Kaisen! I can't tell him that now though. What am I supposed to do? Date him secretly until he gets married and then forget about him? Stop dating him now so it's not weird later on, since we will be around each other forever? My mind raced over my decisions and different scenarios, none of which made me happy.

Harper came and got me for dinner while I was still thinking about what happened. Both, Kaisen and I barely said anything at dinner, only enough for David and Marilyn to think everything was fine. After dinner I hurried to my room so no one could stop to talk to me. I had so many things still racing through my mind.

Chapter 13

"AH," I SCREAMED as I flew up in my bed. Chills ran down my spine as tears streamed down my face. I was crying a lot lately and wasn't sure why. I wiped my eyes with the back of my hand and tried to look around my room for any sign of movement. It was pitched black in my room and I couldn't see anything at all. There was no moon tonight to light my room. I had a nightmare, again.

The man in my dream glided towards me with his arm extended. He grabbed me by the throat and lifted me easily off the ground. I could feel the pressure on my neck as I started to cough. The dream felt so real I thought it had been real until I woke up in my bed.

"Where is it? I know you have it." The evil man started, squeezing my throat tighter as his face got more furious as seconds passed by. "If you won't get it for me, I'll find it myself." He threw me down. My head hit hard against the floor, my body lay limp as my eyes watched the familiar stranger tear apart the room we were in. I couldn't move, talk, or interact at all. I could only watch as the man shuffled through drawers and cupboards. Then I woke up screaming.

"Charlotte?" Kaisen said barreling into my room without knocking. "What's wrong? Are you alright?" Harper ran into my room right after Kaisen. They stood at the edge of my bed staring at me.

"I had another dream about that guy. I think he killed someone." I said as I put my hand on my throat. The dream felt so real that even my neck hurt where he choked me.

"Harper go get mom and David." Kaisen said. After Harper left Kaisen came over and sat next to me on the bed.

"I didn't mean to scream or wake up guys up."

"Its fine, Charlie." I tried not to look at him. I knew that if I looked at him I wouldn't be mad at him anymore. I want to be with him, but I will always know it will end. Why be in a relationship with someone if you know it won't work? "Are you still mad at me?" Ugh, I knew he was going to bring this up. I want to be mad at him, but it's so hard when he is so sweet.

"Kaisen, I don't know." I said in a mean tone. I don't want to hurt him, but if we continue this I'm going to be the one that gets hurt.

"Charlotte, I understand that you are mad at me. You have every right to be, I should have told you before this started. I had many chances while we talked on the phone. I just couldn't tell you. I started liking you the moment we met and as I got to know you the more I liked you."

"But if you knew that you would never end up with me, why would you even try?" I asked.

"I tried to avoid you and make you think I wasn't interested, but it was really hard. I couldn't do it, especially when you would use my own powers on me." He stopped for a few seconds. I didn't know what to say, so I didn't say anything. "Charlotte, if I could change the way I feel about you I would. I didn't mean to hurt you, but I just can't stay away from you." He pauses for a moment. "Will you please say something?"

"Kaisen, I don't know what to say to you right now."

"Just tell me what you are thinking?"

"Okay, well what I'm thinking is that I really want to be with you, but I know if I do, I will get hurt. It's inevitable. We will never have a normal relationship; we will always have to hide it. And in a few months we will have to break up and I'll either love you or hate you, either way we will never be able to be just friends. I know we haven't been together long, but I have liked you from the moment I met you and it's been building since then. I can't just forget that." I stopped to see if he would say anything. He didn't. I don't blame him, I don't know what to say after that either. I looked over at him; he was no longer looking at me. He was staring down into his hands. He looked very young and hurt. It made me mad at myself for doing that to him, I love him, but I know what the right thing to do is. It's break things off, don't continue, and that is what I keep telling myself.

I have to remember to stay strong, don't change my mind, but my mind is walking on a fence between the right thing and the thing that is going to make me happy. I normally do the right thing. I like to walk on the wild side every once in a while. Is this the wild side? It's secretive, which makes it more appealing. It's dangerous which makes it sexy. And it's what will make me happy in this moment and I haven't been this happy in a long time. I have never loved someone like this before; I don't just want to give it up because it will hurt me in the long run. I don't want to think about that. I know the consequences and I know that I can handle them...I think.

We sat in silence while I mentally debated; I came to my decision right as Harper knocked on my door.

Harper, Dad and Marilyn came into my room. I had to fill in the details of my dream that Harper hadn't told them. I told them what I saw in my dream and then I had to describe the office in more detail, so they could figure out the location of my familiar stranger, Bala King. David knew the office that I had been describing. It was Yanie Hergovaben's. Dad quickly called the kingdom to make sure he was alright. Bala King had been there, he killed one of the maids that had been cleaning the office. No one knows what Bala was looking for, but Dad thinks he will keep looking for it, whatever it is. Dad and Marilyn agreed that it would be safer if we cut the trip short and head home tomorrow.

The next morning, I got up early and got dressed. We would probably be leaving early in the afternoon, so I should start packing soon. As I walked down the hall to the kitchen, something outside the window caught my eye. It was snowing out. It looked so pretty with the snow covered pine trees. When I got downstairs Dad and Marilyn were the only two awake.

“Good morning Charlotte.” Dad said.

"Good morning, what time are we planning on leaving?" I asked. It might take longer to get back if it's going to snow all day.

"I don't think we will be able to go home today. There is a bad storm and travel is not advised." Dad said.

"I think I'm going to tell the boys that we aren't leaving so they can sleep in longer." Marilyn said.

"I'll do it." I said, leaving the kitchen before she could say anything. I wanted to talk to Kaisen alone. I went to Harper's room first. I knocked, and then opened up the door. He was lying sprawled out across his bed, his mouth hanging open. "Harper, Harper." I said. I shook him until he made noise. "We aren't going home, we are staying here. There is a big storm and no one is supposed to travel." I told him.

"Okay, thanks." He said rolling over and going back to sleep. I smiled and walked quietly out the door. I knocked on Kaisen's door and he told me to come in.

Kaisen looked up to see who was at the door and opened his eyes wide when he saw me.

"Charlotte? What are you doing here?" He asked as he rubbed his eyes with his hand. He sat up, revealing his bare chest, holy crap he was hot.

"I came to tell you there is a snow storm and we can't leave today."

"Okay." He said. I stood there for a second. "Is there something else?"

"Umh... I can tell you later." I chickened out. "It's early, why don't you go back to sleep." I turned to leave.

"Charlotte, wait." He said. I didn't hear him get out of bed, but before I could reach the door handle he put his hand on my arm. "What is it?" I took a deep breath and turned around. Yikes, he was standing there in just lounge pants. His chest was muscular and beautiful. I took a deep breath and looked up at his face.

"I changed my mind."

"About what?"

"About us. I want to be with you." I said as I took his hand in mine and laced our fingers together.

"Are you sure?" He asked. "What made you change your mind?"

"I changed it last night, right before Harper got there. I always do the right thing no matter if it hurts me or not. This time I will be hurt either way, I just have to decide now or later. Like you said, you can't stay away from me and I can't stay away from you, so why try?" He squeezed my hand in his then dropped my hand and threw his arms around me and hugged me. He stood up straight, lifting me off the ground.

"I didn't mean to hurt you Charlie." he said in my hair.

"I know. I understand." I told him. He put me down and kissed me. "I just don't want to talk about this again until we have to break up, and who knows maybe we will get sick of each other and break up before then." I joked with him.

"I doubt that is going to happen." He said. He pulled my chin up so he could kiss me. His lips were warm and fit perfectly against mine. My stomach started to feel funny and my heart started to beat faster. I loved this feeling, it was intoxicating and wonderful. This is the reason for my decision, because he makes me feel like I have never felt before. I am happy with him and I can't let that go. Kaisen pulled away from the kiss and stared into my eyes.

"Charlotte, I…" He started as a loud knock on the door made us both freeze. What if it was one of our parents? "Hide." Kaisen whispered. I looked around the room as Kaisen walked to the door. I crawled under the bed as far as I could and waited. I heard Kaisen open the door.

"Has Charlotte been in here?" Dad asked.

"Yeah, she told me there is a snow storm and we aren't going home today."

"Alright, just making sure she told you. I came to let you know your mom and I have a lot of work to do after last night. You guys are going to have to find something to do around here until the storm lets up, it's too cold to go outside."

"That's fine. I'll be down for breakfast in a bit."

"That's alright, sleep in if you want." Dad said as I could hear his footsteps and then I heard the sound of a door close.

"You can come out, he is gone." He said. I rolled out from under the bed. "We need to be more careful, that is twice we almost got caught together."

"I know, I need to figure out how to transport like Harper." When I stood up Kaisen pulled me towards him and kissed me.

Chapter 14

THE SNOW STORM lasted two days and as soon as it let up, we left. It took two hours longer to get home because some of the roads hadn't been plowed. We got back home right after lunch time. The original three week vacation turned into ten days. As soon as we arrived Dad and Marilyn went to their offices and started to set up the search for Bala King.

"Do you guys want to go do something?" I asked as we sat around the game room watching TV.

"What did you have in mind?" Harper asked.

"It's not that cold out; we could have an air soft war in the maze."

"Have you ever been in the maze?" Kaisen asked.

"I go in the maze all the time. Why?" I answered.

"Alright, but if we get lost it's your fault." Kaisen said with a smile.

"Ha, I can get through that maze with my eyes closed." I lied. "I have to change into something warmer, I'll be right back."

When I got to my room I noticed my ring glowing on my bedside table. The sun must have been hitting it just right.

"You must be David's daughter, Charlotte." A voice came from behind me as I closed the door. I know this voice, I had heard it before. I turned to find the man from my nightmares standing before me. "I have been watching you for a while and I noticed that you and my son have a thing for each other." He has been watching me? Who is his...? I can't believe I didn't notice this sooner. Bala King is Kaisen and Harper King's father. I couldn't believe that no one told me. I guess it's probably a touchy subject.

"What do you want?" I asked as I stood frozen in the center of the room.

"Forgive me for being rude. I am Balano-Regelnin King, but you can call me Bala." He said extending a hand towards me, thinking I might actually shake it. I just stood there and stared, not sure what to do. Now that I thought about it, Kaisen and Harper do resemble him. They have the same tanned skin, cheek bones and eyebrows. The boys have the same brown eyes, but Bala's are green and look more evil with dark bags.

"Fine, I will skip the formal stuff and head straight to it. I need you to find something for me. I know you can see me in your dreams. I need you to tell me where I can find the Dekian Crystals. I don't wish to be rude but if you don't help me then I will have to bribe you. You wouldn't want something to happen to your new family because you wouldn't help me find my little trinkets, would you?"

"I can't just dream up something on my own. It doesn't work like that. I don't know how I do it."

“That is so disappointing.” He said with an evil look on his face. “I was hoping you would cooperate with me, seeing as you know how it feels to lose someone close to you. I wouldn’t think you would chance feeling that way again.” I thought about everyone that I was close to, and how I felt when my mother died. I can't feel like that again. I won't, I'll help him find whatever it is that he wants, as long as he doesn't hurt anyone.

There was a knock at the door before I could respond to Bala.

“Charlie, are you almost ready?” I heard Kaisen ask through the door. What was I going to do? If I answered him and he came in, Bala might hurt him. But if I don’t answer him, Bala might hurt me, or kidnap me until I find whatever it is he is looking for. He wouldn't hurt his own son, would he? I don't know how to use my powers well enough yet but I have to do something. I looked at Bala, who was standing close enough to me that he could reach me in a few steps if necessary but far enough away that I might be able to reach the door to run away. I looked back to the door. Knock, Knock. “Charlotte?”

Without another hesitation, I sprinted to the door. I could see Bala coming after me from the corner of my eye as I opened the door. “Kaisen, HELP…” I screamed but when Bala reached me he slammed the door shut and locked it, blocking my only exit. Kaisen banged on the door.

“Charlotte, what’s going on?”

“HELP ME, KAISEN. HE'S HERE.” I shouted, hoping he knew what that meant. Bala came towards me, grabbing me by my throat, just like in my dream. He lifted me up so I couldn’t scream or get away. I could barely breathe and the sharp pressure on my throat made me want to cough. I tried to kick him but I could barely move, it was like he was controlling me from moving. I could hear Kaisen continue to bang on the door as loud as he could.

"That wasn't smart, Miss Charlotte." Bala said, ignoring Kaisen.

I grabbed at Bala's hand around my throat and tried to pry it off, it wasn't working. I tried to scream, but only tiny groans came out. I could barely breathe; I knew I was going to pass out soon if he didn't put me down. I thrashed around as best I could. I tried to kick my legs at him, but couldn't kick him hard enough; I could feel myself start to slip away. I just noticed that the banging on the door had subsided when Harper and Kaisen transported into my room. Bala had been saying something to me, but I was preoccupied with trying to get away that I wasn't listening.

"I am going to have to…" Bala was saying.

"Put her down." Kaisen said, I could tell he was trying to persuade Bala to do as he wanted. I could also tell that Bala was very strong minded and it didn't take much for him to ignore Kaisen's demand.

Bala threw me across the room into one of my tables. "Where is it, Kaisen?" Bala sneered.

"Where is what?" Kaisen screamed at him.

"Your crystal?" Bala said as he glared down at Kaisen as he walked towards him. I watched Kaisen as Harper came to my side and threw his arms around me and tried transporting me. I watched as the room blurred and faded, then before I could close my eyes we were standing in the hall. "I'm sorry; this is as far as I could take you. I haven't seen him in so long and I panicked." He said as he took my hand and pulled me quickly down the hall.

"I can't believe you didn't tell me he was your father." I started. "We can't just leave Kaisen in there alone. What if Bala tries to hurt him?"

"Kaisen can take care of himself." Harper said as he stopped a few yards from my door he threw his arms around me again and transported us to David's office.

"Go get your dad, I'll get my mom. They will know what to do." Harper said. We met back with our parents out in the hall a few seconds later.

"Kaisen is trying to keep Bala in Charlotte's room long enough for me to get her away and get you guys in there to capture him so you can take him back to Zweb." Harper told our parents before Marilyn transported David upstairs.

"Harper, take me up there." I told him as I tried to gasp for air, my throat was hurting so bad now.

By the time Harper transported me up to my room, Bala was gone and Kaisen was passed out on the floor. He wasn't hurt bad; Bala knocked him out so he could escape. I was so angry with myself, what could I have done differently so my family wasn't in danger? What can I do now to keep them safe from Bala King? I didn't know why he wanted my help. I barely know anything about Andeka or the crystals he was talking about. Maybe that's why he wants me to help him, I have crazy dreams that end up real and I don't know enough about Andeka to know what the crystals can do, so I won't feel bad getting them for him, as long as I can keep my family safe.

"Don't worry, Charlotte. We will find him and he won't be able to hurt you or anyone else." Dad told me. I wasn't worried about myself at this point. I was worried about everyone else. Bala was right; I could never live through the feeling of losing someone again. I can't let myself be responsible for something like that. I need to find out how to use my powers so I can do what I can.

"What are Dekian Crystals?" I asked Marilyn.

"How did you hear about them?" She seemed shocked.

"That is what Bala wants from me, to dream about him finding the crystals."

"That doesn't make sense, you don't make your dreams happen, Charlotte, you dream about things that have happened. I don't think you can do that. You don't choose the turn out."

"I know that, but that's what he thinks. What are Dekian Crystals and what do they do?" I asked again.

"Dekian Crystals are very rare stones; there are only six colors that we know of. Each color does something different. Emerald crystals are used for protection. The red crystals are used to strengthen a Cigam's gifts. There is only one blue and one purple. Whoever has the blue crystal can't be subjected to any other Cigam's powers, unless willing. The purple crystal absorbs some of the talents of Cigam that use their talents while holding onto the crystal. It can also carry around all that power and the Cigam in control of the crystal can use all that power against anyone. Yellow glows when the person wearing it lies and the Orange one makes people forget what they are doing. All of the crystals are equally powerful and are often camouflaged to resemble jewelry so that Cigam can use them undetected, but that is kind of hard, seeing as the crystals let off a glow when they are used. I actually have one of the crystals. I always wear it." She said as she showed her emerald pendant necklace. "Most of the rulers have the crystals but the purple crystal and the blue crystal were hidden when Bala King first went to jail."

"What did he go to jail for the first time?" I asked.

"I think you should ask your dad that." She said then left the room without another word.

"BALA KING WAS put in jail when he went crazy and wanted to be Supreme Ruler of Andeka." Dad explained. "He killed six people, the rulers of Andeka and their spouse. He killed your aunt and uncle, Darius and Grace Callaway, that's when I had to leave you when you were a toddler. I had to come rule his part of the kingdom, since I was the next in line. He also killed The Ruler of the Flink, which had left no heir, so Guin-Bock appointed new rulers, Patricia and Glen Darby. Bala, also, killed his parents, Julio and Auroa King, rulers of the Che kingdom, leaving no one to rule that kingdom either. A distant relative came to take over the thrown, Yanie Hergovaben. Marilyn and Bala were the rulers of the last kingdom. Marilyn's parents passed away at a young age so she got the kingdom. Some think that Bala killed her parents as well, but he was never caught. But, he snuck into each castle and killed them all within one night. The morning after that he came to Marilyn, who was pregnant with Harper at the time. He wanted her to join him but she wouldn't do it. She tried to fight him off after he tried to kill her and Kaisen. Marilyn transported

Kaisen and herself to a safe location while Bala was being locked up.

"I came to Andeka to take over the thrown and I ruled it alone for thirteen years, then to make the kingdom stronger, I agreed to an arranged marriage to Marilyn, and I fell in love with her. Kaisen is betrothed too, did he ever tell you that? I don't think he is happy about it, but Marilyn did it so that if something happened to her, he would be taken care of by the girl's parents. You have actually met the girl Kaisen is going to marry; you went tubing with her and her brother."

"I know, Dad. Kaisen told me already. So, is Harper betrothed to?" I asked.

"No, he is second in line for the thrown. If something happened to Kaisen, Harper would rule. I actually need to talk to you about his." He said. "As you learn about the powers and rulers of Andeka, you will be given a choice. You are my only child and you are the sole heir to my kingdom. If you want it when I step down, you will have the option to rule it. If you don't want to rule it, you can chose to give it to Kaisen and keep it as one large kingdom or you can divide it from Kaisen's and give it to Harper." Do I want to rule my own kingdom? I wasn't sure at all. I don't want to now but maybe I'll want to in the future.

"As of right now, I don't want it, but I want to learn my powers and then maybe after I go to college I can see if I change my mind." I told him.

"That is perfectly fine, Charlotte, I didn't expect you to want it after what happened today. Besides you have a long time to think about it. You have to be married to rule a kingdom."

"But you weren't married and neither was Marilyn." I said confused.

"Technically I was married when I became ruler. I was married to your mother even though she was never there. She asked for the divorce while I was ruler and I went in front of Guin-Bock and asked to rule for a while on my own, since I had done it well for a few years, he didn't see a problem. Marilyn was still married, too. Bala King was in jail and had tried to kill Marilyn but they were technically still married. When Bala king escaped the first time he came after Marilyn. That is when Guin-Bock and Marilyn's parents convinced her she needed to have someone to take care of her and the boys. She agreed and Guin-Bock requested I do it. I needed to have someone to sit by my side to help me rule also, it was almost too perfect for us. I had kept you a secret from everyone except my parents, of course. So, I needed an heir to my thrown anyways. Combining two quarters of Andeka was hard, because it hasn't ever been done before and it puts a larger target on us, since we have twice the power and land as the other two quarters, but it makes us stronger. We get along with the other Rulers and Guin-Bock would never let anything get out of hand, but with Bala King on the run, anything could happen.

"The Cigam aren't the only ones who are powerful in Andeka, there are many other living creatures that are just as eager to take over as rulers of Andeka. And Bala King knows it, he could easily persuade them to build an army and start a war with the Cigam. I just hope he is too ignorant for that kind of thinking."

I hoped the same thing; I didn't want to think about a war. I wasted the rest of the week with Kaisen and Harper, sitting around, playing games. We were supposed to stay inside. Marilyn put guards at every entrance and exit of the house. Bala was not a Bain and was not able to transport into the house unless someone was working with him. No one saw him with anyone ever, so we assumed he was working alone, like he did the first time he broke out of Zweb.

"KAISEN ARE YOU alright?" I asked as Kaisen walked by me without saying anything. It was like he was in a trance. He shook his head and came out of it.

"I'm fine, Charlotte. I'm just feeling a little strange, that's all." He said as he picked up my hand and kissed it. "Will you go with me to the maze today after lunch?"

"We aren't supposed to go outside, Kaisen."

"It'll be fine. No one has seen Bala in days. Please? I want to show you something." He asked again, giving me the sweetest smile.

"Okay," I agreed.

Kaisen was acting strange all day and I wasn't sure why. He was saying things in a weird way and doing things that he doesn't normally do. And at times he would seem really upset and other times he would seem really happy. It was not normal at all. I kept asking him if he was alright and he told me he was fine. I didn't believe him but I didn't press his mood further.

I felt extra strange in the maze tonight, not just because the way Kaisen was acting but I couldn't help feel like we were being watched, yet no one was around. I was starting to think I was becoming paranoid. I felt like something was wrong, but I couldn't figure out what.

Kaisen was starting to worry me when he didn't want to hold my hand while we walked. He usually made any excuse to be close to me, and I liked it that way. He snapped at me a few different times also. I knew something was wrong with him so I tried not to let his actions bother me. Harper was playing video games and I knew he wasn't going to look at his phone any time soon, but I text him anyways. 'Kaisen is acting strange, have your phone on you if I call. We are out in the maze.' I read over the text and pressed send.

"Kaisen, dance with me?" I asked playfully, trying to cheer him up. I pulled his hand with me as I walked under the gazebo in an open section in the center of the maze. He pulled away from me.

"I don't want to dance." He snapped.

"Hon is there something wrong, you seem angry at me. Did I do something wrong?"

"What don't you do wrong?" He said, catching me off guard. He had never said anything like this to me before.

"Excuse me? What did I do?" I was upset now.

"Nothing, just forget it." He said with an angry glare, and then as I watched his scary expression, it changed. His features thawed from his icy stare and he because the old Kaisen. "I'm sorry. I don't know what has gotten into me. I didn't mean to say those things. I am not myself today, I feel…strange, like someone else is running my mind. Forgive me. I would love to dance with you."

I was a little frightened by his behavior and wasn't sure if I wanted to be alone with him anymore. Maybe he had severe bi-polar disorder or something. "No, it's alright. I don't want to dance. We should probably get back anyways."

"Charlotte, I said I was sorry." He said, still trying to be nice but I could tell the nice Kaisen was gone and the mean one was in his place. "Dance with me. I know you want to dance, you just said so."

"I changed my mind; I just want to go back inside… I'm thirsty." I lied, trying to get away from him. This was no longer Kaisen, it was someone else. He reminded me of Bala the night he was in my room.

Kaisen walked towards me and grabbed onto my arms. "Dance with me." He pushed me up against one of the poles on the gazebo. I was really frightened now; his grip on my arm was tight. His hand was in just the right spot on my bracelet that the red crystal charm was digging into my skin.

"Kaisen, please let go of me." I asked. He glared at me and gave me a weird look. He didn't let go of me, but tightened his grip. "What is wrong with you?"

"I don't love you, and I don't think I ever really did. You're just not… what I want and you can never be…" Kaisen stopped mid-sentence as the tears fell from my face. For a split second Kaisen's face melted back to himself. "Charlotte, help me." Kaisen said. It was apparent now that Kaisen was being controlled by someone else. He wasn't trying to hurt me; someone else was speaking for him. I could tell by the changes in his facial expressions.

"You don't love me?" I sobbed, my heart broken. Even though I knew it wasn't his words, but they were still coming from his mouth, in his voice.

"I didn't mean what I said… I never loved you. How could I love someone like you? How did you ever think that, couldn't you tell I was lying? I am pretty good at persuasion, I guess." At that point I knew that it was Bala saying things with Kaisen's mouth. Kaisen has never told me he loves me. Why would he say that he didn't mean what he said if he has never said it?

I could see Bala King in Kaisen's eyes now. I wasn't sure how to handle this madness. How close could Bala be for him to control Kaisen so completely. I utterly and completely believed Bala, that was the sad part… I believed that Kaisen didn't love me. No Charlotte, think about it I told myself. Kaisen would never say this. Besides he has been acting strange all day.

"I don't understand." I tried to tell him, but Kaisen (Bala) laughed in my face. He loosened his grip on my arms and my bracelet was no longer cutting into my arm. I looked down at my wrist to see if the bracelet had cut into my skin, I could only see my red crystal charm glowing... Crap. Marilyn told me about the crystals, that they glow when they are being used. I still don't know how to use my powers much at all, but somehow my crystal is glowing. I didn't know until now that it was one that Marilyn had mentioned. If I could only remember what the red one meant.

"I never want to see you again, Charlotte. Don't follow me." Kaisen backed away from me and left the gazebo and walked out of sight onto one of the pathways of the maze. I wasn't sure why, but I followed him. I didn't want to be near him but I couldn't help think that something was up. I waited a few moments before turning the corner onto the path so he wouldn't know I was following him. I heard a strange noise coming from down the path, it sounded like someone grunted then a loud thud followed by rustling of the hedges. It had to have been Kaisen; I was scared to find out though.

As I followed him I tried to remember what the crystal meant. I know that green is for protection... damn... That is probably why my grandmother gave me that ring. It was glowing when I got into my room because it was warning me. That was the day Bala was in my room.

I turned another corner in the maze, but no one was there, I walked down the long straight pathway and came to another turn. There was nothing down this path either, I kept going though. I heard the strange noise again, this time it was louder and I could tell the grunting sound was Kaisen. I quickened my pace, then after hearing the noise a third time I started to run. I came around the corner at a dead sprint and saw Kaisen lying at the end of the path. I wasn't sure what was wrong with him, but I knew he was hurt. I pulled my phone from my pocket and dialed Harper.

"Hey, we are in the maze, something is wrong with Kaisen can you come get us please? I think Bala might be out here." I asked. "I'm not sure where we are exactly, sort of by the open area with the gazebo. Please hurry and when you get here, be careful." I hung up the phone and walked slowly to Kaisen, searching for something that would explain why he was on the ground, maybe a trip string or something.

"Kaisen are you alright?" I asked, still trying to keep my distance in case he turned on me. There was a small egg shaped rock on the ground next to Kaisen. It was a light blue color. "What is that?" I pointed at the weird rock. I bent down to pick it up when Kaisen opened his eyes and saw what I was talking about.

"Don't touch that. It's been hexed. See." He touched it and his body jolted and he let out a loud grunting sound again.

"Kaisen!" I cried. I didn't want him to be hurt, I couldn't stand watching that. "Are you alright?" I knelt down beside him.

"Yes and no. Bala is here. He used that to control me." He explained as he pointed to the hexed ball. "It's a Hue-Orb. It can control the mind." He sat up and looked into my eyes, and I knew he was telling the truth.

"And that's why you were acting strange? And that's why you…"

"I'm so sorry." He sighed, hanging his head, breaking our eye contact. "Will you forgive me for all of the terrible things I said and did to you? I didn't know what I was doing; I swear I would never ever hurt you like that on purpose." Kaisen said as he held my hands in his. He didn't give me time to respond.

"Charlotte, I don't know what I would do without you, you mean so much to me. I don't know how to explain it, other than..." He took a minute to gather his thoughts. "Every time I think about you my hands shake, and every time you walk into the room, my stomach feels empty and achy, in a good way. And when you look at me," he started as he lifted my chin up, so I would look him in the eyes, "I can barely breathe. My heart starts to race and my legs start to shake and I can't look away… it's like you have complete control over me. I am intoxicated from the way you make me feel, all the time. I hate being away from you. David would kill me if he knew how I felt about you. I know it shouldn't matter what anyone thinks, but it does, because no matter how much I want to, I can't always be with you.

"Charlotte, I have never cared for, worried about, or thought about someone so much in my life, until I met you. If anything happened to you, I don't know what I would do. You know I would never hurt you on purpose. Charlotte, I... love you." Pulling my hands closer to him, he kept my gaze as he continued. That was the first time he had said those words to me. I almost thought he had said something else until he said them again. "Charlotte I love you, I love you more than anything in the world. I would give anything in the world for you. I would give you anything in the world that I could offer. I don't know how better to explain myself, I have never felt this way before and I'm so scared that you don't feel as strongly or the same way. After how I treated you, I don't know how you could…" I stopped him by pulling my hands away from him and placing one of my hands over his mouth.

"Stop. How can you say that? Kaisen, I am shocked at you. I have never heard anyone tell me exactly how they feel about me, when I couldn't have expressed it in any different words. I don't even know if what I just said made any sense to you, but what I'm trying to say is that… I love you, too. I am so in love with you, Kaisen." Kaisen pulled my chin up to his face and kissed me. I wrapped my arms around him and he winced. I let go right away. “Are you alright?”

“Yeah, I'm fine. But we need to find Bala. I'm sure he is here somewhere.” Kaisen said as he gave me a quick peck on the lips.

“Uh, hum.” A voice cleared making us both jump. Bala King was standing behind Harper, holding him around his throat. “Sorry to interrupt but I think I have something you want.” Kaisen pulled me close to his side.

“Let Harper go.” Kaisen demanded, but Bala just laughed.

“Do you have what I want?” He asked.

“No, but give us Harper and we will help you find it,” Kaisen said.

“How stupid do you think I am? You bring me the crystal and you can have your brother back.” Kaisen glared at him and started inching towards them. Bala King pulled out an orb from his pocket and held it towards Kaisen. I recognized it right away. It was the same as the one lying on the ground.

“Stay back Kaisen, I wouldn’t want to hurt you or Charlotte. Now, I’m taking your brother until you get me what belongs to me.”

“I don’t know what you are talking about. I don’t have anything of yours.” Kaisen objected still moving towards them as slowly as he can.

“Where is the Crimson Current? I know you have it.” Bala accused.

“I don't know what you mean.” Kaisen said.

“The red crystal. Where is it?” Bala barked.

“I don’t have it anymore.”

"What do you mean you don't have it anymore? That was a powerful crystal, are you brainless?" Bala said in outrage.

"I guess I must be because I seriously don't have it anymore." Kaisen explained.

"Where is it then?"

Kaisen debated the question and finally answered. "It's is a safe place."

Bala immediately looked at me. "She has it doesn't she?"

"No," Kaisen said unconvincingly. I slowly moved my arm with my bracelet behind my back, trying not to look suspicious. Bala wasn't convinced and he noticed me moving. He started towards us. "She doesn't have it." Kaisen lied, again, this time more believable. Kaisen was almost close enough to them now that he could take a few long steps and reach them.

"Charlotte, give me the crystal." Bala ignored Kaisen. Bala was so persuasive, it took all of my will power not to pull the bracelet off and hand it to him. I knew he was using his powers on me and I had to use all of my strength to restrain myself. Then I remembered what the charm did. It strengthens a Cigam's powers.

"I… I don't know what you're talking about. I don't have it." I said. "Maybe you should go find it for yourself."

"Maybe you should hand it over or you will never see Harper again." He threatened. I was hoping that was a bluff.

"I can't hand something over I don't have." I yelled, convincing myself now that I didn't have it even though the tiny charm weighed a ton on my wrist.

"Then maybe you should find it for me and then you can hand it over. Either way, you're going to get it for me. So, you can either hand it over now or else." He threatened again.

"Or else what?" Kaisen yelled taking a step forward.

Bala gave him an evil grin. "Harper, take us, now." Bala demanded, still holding Harper around the neck. Harper let out a soft moan as he closed his eyes in pain.

"No," Kaisen said. He lunged forward trying to stop them from leaving. I stood frozen when I watched all three of them disappear, leaving me alone in the maze. NO! They are gone! What was I supposed to do now? I looked down at my beaming red crystal. I should have just given it to him in the first place. I didn't know where they were and how was I supposed to get to them? The only thing I could do was tell Dad. He would know what to do… I think. I tried to keep my mind from wandering as I ran back to the house as fast as I could. I had made such a mess of things. My eyes were watering as I came up to Dad's office. I didn't know how I was going to tell him that Kaisen and Harper are gone. This is all my fault. My emotions were so uncontrolled that when I ran into his office to tell him what happened I burst into tears.

Chapter 15

After he got me to call down enough for him to understand what I was saying, I told him everything about what happened. I showed Dad the crystal on my bracelet and told him that I had received it as a gift and I didn’t know it was special. I didn't tell him who gave it to me and he didn't ask. I can’t believe that Kaisen would give me something so valuable.

“Has Bala seen the crystal?” Dad asked.

“No, I don't think he knows what it looks like.” I said, knowing what he meant.

“How are you supposed to get the crystal to him?”

“I have no idea. He never said. They just left.” I said.

“Don't worry Charlotte, we will find them.” He said as he kissed my forehead.

He made me stay in his office while he went to tell Marilyn what had happened. Fortunately she wasn't in her office to hear me cry about how I lost her sons. I overheard them in the hall. I started to cry again as I peeked through the crack in the door. When he told her, her face went pale and she almost fell to her knees as she started to cry. My dad caught her and sat her down on the floor as he held onto her.

"No. He can't have them. He can't." She cried. "David, he tried to kill them last time. They were just little babies and he tried to kill them. What do you think he will do to them now?"

THEY SEARCHED FOR the boys for almost a week without any sign of them. After the first night without finding them I couldn't cry about it anymore. I was to mad to cry. I wanted to help get them back however I could. Dad wouldn't let me help search, he told me that I would be more in the way than helpful. He told me to just wait to hear news. Well I couldn't wait any longer. I started practicing my powers all day and as long as I could stay awake at night. I had Harriett come over and help me with calming one day. Then I had Jessie and Connor come over and teach me their mild form of persuasion. I even called Lex. I needed as much help as I could get. He taught me how to transport myself. I practiced and practiced for days. The crystals really helped, too. I put on my green crystal ring and never took it off, same with my bracelet. I wanted to be ready. I was starting to get the hang of the few powers that my friends helped me with. I could transport myself to different areas of the house. I couldn't take any one with me, but at least I was learning. I would practice persuasion on Marilyn. I would ask her for outrageous things and eventually it was easy for me to get her to say yes. Marilyn knew that I was practicing and when she got upset or overwhelmed she would let me try to calm her. My powers started to work every time I would try to use them. I would follow my dad around when he was at home so I could feed off of his powers. I wanted to get as good as I could at persuasion.

After searching for the boys for six days my pocket buzzed and started singing Harper's ring tone. I flipped open the screen and read the message out loud. "We are waiting for you in Glyrus Forest. Traveling east into the forest after the third light turn left, we will be in the house on the right. Bring the crystal. Make sure you come alone."

I took my phone straight to my dad and told him what it said.

"You're not going. I'll take it to him." David insisted. I knew fighting wouldn't change his answer so I started to remove my crystal from my bracelet. "Keep it, I have a fake one I can give him, he won't know the difference."

'David will bring it to him. No one else will come with him. He doesn't want me to come.' I text back.

'I won't accept the crystal from anyone else but you, Charlotte.' I read the text to David.

"Why? Ask him why it matters who gives him the crystal as long as he gets it?" David told me.

"No more questions! If you want to see Harper and Kaisen again, send Charlotte tomorrow night." I read the responding text message.

"There is no way I'm sending you alone." He told me furiously. "I'll go myself and try to make a deal with him." He said as he pulled out a lock box from his drawer.

"What are you doing?" I asked.

"I have this." He said as he pulled out a red glowing crystal from the box. "It's a fake and it glows when someone touches it.

He will never know the difference." I watched as Dad pulled out a gun from the lock box and set it down on the desk and pulled out a clip from the box. He slowly loaded the clip.

"Dad you're not going to kill him are you?" I asked.

"If I get the shot, I'm going to take it. He has done too much harm in this world, Charlotte. As a ruler, I have the power to make this decision." Dad is going to ruin everything if he shows up and tries to shoot Bala. What if there are others there also? He could put Kaisen and Harper in more danger than they already are.

I saw that there is a third item in the lock box. It is an orb, similar to the one that was controlling Kaisen. "Dad what does that do?" I asked.

"This is a Bain-Orb. It will take a Non-Bain Cigam anywhere they want to go. It will take multiple Cigam if used by a Bain." He said.

"Is that how you are planning on getting there?" I asked.

"No, I have a GPS in my car programmed for Andeka. I will set the coordinates tomorrow night when I go over there."

"Dad, are you sure you want to go alone, isn't it dangerous?" I asked.

"It won't be that dangerous if I do this correctly."

"So what are you going to do?"

"I'm going to go in there and show him the crystal, then once he has it I will pull the gun on him and shoot him. Then I will get Kaisen and Harper out of there. It shouldn't be that hard once I find them."

"Are you taking anyone with you?"

"I'll have someone wait in the car so if something happens they can come help me. Honey, you don't have anything to worry about, I will be fine."

"I know, Dad. I love you." I said as I hugged him, taking the lock box key off of the desk as he wasn't looking. He doesn't need it to lock it, just to unlock it. I held the key in my hand while he put the prepared gun back into the lock box.

"Well, Charlotte, we both had a long day, I'm just glad we will have the boys back tomorrow night. I need to get to bed. See you in the morning." He said as he kissed my forehead and walked off to bed. I started to walk towards my room and stopped when he was in his room. I walked back to his office and closed the door quietly behind me. I didn't turn on the light just in case he walked back by. I pulled out my phone and turned on the flashlight app. I used it to guide my way. I unlocked the box and took out all three things from it: the gun, the orb and the fake crystal. I checked the safety, making sure it was on, then placed the gun in the front of my pants and pulled my shirt over it. Then I placed the other two items in my pockets. I closed the box and laid the key back on the desk. I won't need it, because when I get back Dad will know what I did. He will know I took these things. I hope to be back before the night is over. What I didn't tell him was that the text I got from Harper's phone said tonight, not tomorrow night. I knew he wouldn't want me to go. I just needed to know his plan so that I could steal it. Damn, I'm turning into a delinquent. I thought to myself. I went up to my room and changed my clothes. I put on a hooded sweatshirt that had a large front pocket to hide the gun. I tucked in my bracelet so that he wouldn't be able to see it and put the crystal in one pocket and the orb in the other pocket. I snuck outside to the garage and pulled Dad's car keys from his key holder. I was breaking so many rules tonight; I would be grounded for sure. I set the gun on the seat next to me; I couldn't drive with it in my pocket. Once I set Dad's GPS, I text the boys.

'I'm on my way.'

'Are you alone?'

'Yes, and I have the crystal. Are Kaisen and Harper alright?'

'Just get here.' I did as the message instructed. It took twenty-five minutes for me to get to the entrance to the forest. I watched for lights, I was in the middle of nowhere. After ten minutes of driving around in the pitch black night, I saw a small bright light. It was a permanent camp fire with a few tents set up. I kept driving. One light down two to go. The next light was a house. Then the third light was a street light. This was the first and only street light I had seen in the forest. It felt strange to have one street light in the middle of a forest. I kept going. It took forever to get to the next road. I turned left, then drove down the road for a mile and came to a small log style house. The two lights on the main floor were on but nothing else. I took the gun from the seat next to me, checked the safety and locked the clip in place. I tucked it into my sweatshirt and readjusted the sleeves over my wrists, hiding my bracelet. My green ring was glowing and was easy to spot. I tucked it into my pocket, opposite of the fake crystal. I took a deep breath. This was it; I'm going to get Kaisen and Harper back. I hoped they were alright.

I walked up to the door and knocked. My heart was pounding, I wasn't sure what to expect. And I was terrified. Bala opened the door slowly.

"Come in." He said in a demanding voice. After I was inside he took a step out glancing around for anyone else that I might have brought with me and then he stepped back inside, closing and locking the door behind him. "Did you bring the crystal?"

"Yes." I said as I pulled the fake crystal from my pocket and held it up for him to see. It was glowing and seemed like the real deal. It looked almost identical to mine, except this one didn't have a charm clasp on it. Bala held his hand out for it, but I pulled it back in and shoved it back into my pocket. "No. You can't have it until I get Harper and Kaisen."

"They are in here." He motioned for me to enter another door behind him. "After you."

I walked into the room and looked around for the boys. They were sitting next to each other. Harper was tied with each arm attached to something heavy, probably so he couldn't transport himself and the objects anywhere. Kaisen was tied with his hands together. He was slumped over in his seat, head down and motionless. I ran over to them and threw my arms around them.

"Are you alright?" I asked them. I pulled Kaisen's head up to mine to see if he was alright.

"They are fine. Now let me have the crystal."

"Not until you release them and let us all walk out of here." I said turning to Bala. He was furious. He walked towards me and grabbed me by the throat.

"You are really starting to get on my nerves." He spat. I couldn't speak, his grip on my throat was too tight.

"Let her go, please." I could hear Kaisen say from behind me, the pain in his voice surprised me and I tried to look at him. He sounded like he had been crying or that he still was. Bala released my throat but held on to my shirt as he smacked Kaisen in the mouth. I could tell this wasn't the first time he had hit him. I saw Kaisen's lip was already busted open and there was dried blood on the outside of his bottom lip. I also noticed his neck was bruised. He hadn't been crying, it hurt his throat to talk.

"I'm only going to ask nicely one more time. Let me have the crystal." I glanced at Kaisen and Harper and took a deep sigh as I reached into the pocket of my sweatshirt. I pulled away from Bala hard and he lost the grasp of my shirt. I backed up towards the boys again as I pulled out the hand gun Dad had given me. I pointed it at Bala.

"Now you listen and you listen well. I'll give you the damn crystal when you let Harper and Kaisen go." I was trying to act tough, but I could feel my legs shake under me and I was terrified as I waited for Bala's reaction.

"No one needs to get hurt here Charlotte." Bala said raising his hands up but I could tell he wasn't scared of me. I needed to make him believe that I could actually kill him, even if I didn't believe I would.

"Shut up!" I screamed. A tear fell down my cheek. "Untie them now." I said moving to the side unblocking them from Bala. "Now!" I said again, lifting the gun in the air and flipping the safety and pulling the trigger. The gun let out a loud noise and the force of the gun made me stumble. I flipped the safety back on and pointed it back at Bala. He jumped forward, flipping out a knife and cutting Kaisen's ropes, freeing his hands. Kaisen got up and came to stand behind me. He made a motion with his hands to see if I wanted him to take the gun for me. I shook him off and kept my eyes on Bala. He was cutting Harper free. As Harper got up Bala grabbed him, wrapping his arm around him like before and raised the knife to his throat.

"Now, give me the crystal." He demanded again.

I took one hand off the gun raising both hands in the air, letting the gun rest in my hand. I pushed my hand down into my pocket and pulled out the crystal. I held it between my two fingers. "I'm going to place it on the table, alright? Please don't hurt him." I set the crystal on the table next to Kaisen and I. "We are walking away now. We are going to walk to the door. Just let Harper go."

"If I let him go, how do I know you aren't going to shoot me?" Bala sneered.

"You don't, but I'm not a murderer, you are. I just want to get out of here and never see you again." I said.

Bala grinned and said, "You probably don't know how to shoot that thing anyways." He released Harper.

Once Harper was out of the way and Bala picked up the crystal, I raised my gun again. I had the shot and I knew I wouldn't miss. I never dreamed in a million years I would have to shoot anyone. I was shaking and tears streamed down my face.

"Bala?" He turned towards me enough where I could get a shot at the middle of his chest. I took a deep breath, flipped off the safety, closed my eyes and pulled the trigger. The jolt of the gun pushed me into Kaisen. My eyes flew open and I watched as blood stained Bala's shirt. I had shot him in the stomach on the left side of his body. I gasped, I knew I had shot him but I still couldn't believe it. Bala fell down onto the floor. I was bawling now. "Oh my god." I was shaking as I pushed the safety back on the gun. I didn't know what to do with it. I had just shot someone with this weapon and he was going to die because of me. I didn't want to touch the gun or even see it ever again. I held the gun out as far away from my body as I could.

"Charlotte," Kaisen shook my arm. "Let me have that." He took the gun from me then I felt my knees lock up and I got light headed. Did I really just shoot someone? I was going to need serious therapy after this, I thought to myself. "We need to go." Kaisen said. He towed me out of the house by my arm. I got into the driver's seat as I sobbed. I started the car and drove off as fast as I could, peeling out of the driveway.

"I shot him." I finally said, sobbing.

"Charlotte, it's going to be alright." Kaisen winced as he tried to speak. My eyes started to gush water and the road started to get blurry, I wiped my eyes and pulled over to the side of the road a few miles from the lodge. I put my head against the steering wheel and sobbed more.

"Charlotte, it's alright. You did what you had to do to keep us safe." Harper said from the back seat. He squeezed my shoulder and Kaisen put his hand over my hand.

"Harper, do you feel alright to drive?" Kaisen asked.

"Yeah, I..." Harper started.

"No..." I objected. "I can drive, just give me a second."

"Charlotte, please, I'm fine. I promise." He said getting out of the car and opening up my door. I unbuckled my seat belt and got out.

"Thank you." I said as I wrapped my arms around Harper and hugged him. "I'm glad you're alright." I said into his shoulder. He let out a small laugh.

"Thank you for saving my life, again." He said back. I let go of him and got into the back seat. Kaisen had climbed into the back seat, too. Once I shut my door, I pulled him in for a hug as well.

"Are you alright?" I asked him.

"I'm fine. Thank you for coming to get us. I love you." He said. My stomach fluttered and made tears stream from my face a little more.

"I love you too." I said. "Kaisen, I shot him." I sobbed in his arms.

"Sh..." Kaisen tried to calm me down.

I felt terrible, no matter how evil Bala was, no matter how many people he killed, I hoped he wouldn't die. I didn't want to be a murderer like him. He was Kaisen and Harper's father. I just shot their dad. My mom's death was an accident but if it was murder I wouldn't have been able to get over it. "I am so sorry. I should have let him walk away. I'm so sorry." I cried into Kaisen's shirt, not knowing if he could understand my blubbering or not.

"Shh… Charlotte, it's alright." He stroked my hair.

"No, it's not. That's your father and I just shot him. How can you ever love a murderer?"

"I can't." He said, I rubbed my eyes and sat up. "He may be biologically my father but he kidnapped us and he tried to kill us Charlotte, and if you hadn't have shot him he might not have let us leave and he would try to kill us again. He would have killed us all. It's self-defense Charlotte. You saved our lives." He tried to explain. I thought that was a load of crap. How can someone say that I didn't murder him? I shot him with a gun and he is dead, that is murder, no matter what. Not thinking about it until right now, I pulled my phone out and called Dad.

"Hello?" Dad answered half asleep. I was in a world of trouble.

"Dad, its Charlotte. I took your gun and the orb and the fake red crystal from the lock box. And I stole your car with the GPS and I tracked down Kaisen and Harper." I told him, trying to hold back the tears as best as I could.

"You did WHAT?" He yelled into the phone, wide awake now. "Are you alright?" He asked. "Did you find the boys?"

"Yes, they are fine, I have them with me and we are heading back now. I am sorry I lied and stole from you, but Dad, Bala only wanted me to come get them. He would have hurt you. I knew what I was doing, I swear."

"Charlotte..."

"Dad, I shot him. I shot Bala." I sobbed into the phone. "We just left him there to die. I can't believe I shot him. I think I killed him, Dad. I killed him." I was devastated.

"Charlotte, it's going to be alright, honey. Just please get home safely." He said.

"We will, I have to hang up now, we will be home shortly. Dad, please don't be mad at me." I said as I hung up the phone.

When we made it home, Dad and Marilyn were waiting right by the door. They hugged and kissed us, and Marilyn cried.

When they finally got me to calm down David and Marilyn sent the boys to bed while they sat me down to talk about what happened. They tried to explain that what I did wasn't murder, that I was protecting my family and that it was necessary to come back unharmed. I wanted to feel better about what happened. What they said was reassuring but it was still hard for me to believe that what I did was right. They didn't ground me for taking off, but I knew that if I had done that for any other reason, I would have been.

After I went up to my room, I laid in bed for about two hours thinking while I stared at the ceiling. Someone knocked on my door but I didn't want to answer. Whoever it was didn't want to come in, they just left. About twenty minutes later someone knocked on my door again. “Charlotte? Are you awake?” Kaisen asked as he poked his head inside my room.

“Yes, you can come in.”

“Why didn't you answer your door?”

“I didn't want to get up in case it was your mom or my dad.” He laughed a little, then locked my door and came to lay by me on my bed.

“I can't sleep.” I said as I turned towards him. He pulled me to him and held me. “I can’t think about anything except pulling the trigger earlier.”

“Honey, don’t think about it anymore. David came by a bit ago; he said you didn't answer the door when he knocked. When they went back to that house, Bala was gone.” He told me. I didn't know what that meant. “They didn't find drag marks and they checked the woods around the house, they couldn't find him.

“So that means I didn’t kill anyone?” I asked hopeful.

“You didn’t kill anyone.” He laughed, kissing my forehead.

“Thank God. I felt so bad. I never want to take a life. I don’t know how people can shoot other people. It’s the worst feeling in the world.” I laid my head on his shoulder.

“Well, just don’t think about it anymore. Now all we have to worry about it Bala coming back to get revenge because you shot him.” Kaisen warned. He watched my expression as my eyes got big with worry. “I’m joking, Charlie, calm down. I won’t let anything happen to you, I promise.”

“I believe you.” I said with a yawn.

“Get some sleep; everything is going to be fine.”

“You can't sleep here, what if Marilyn or my Dad catches us?”

“Don’t worry so much. No one is going to find out. They will probably let us sleep in since it’s so late and we all had a rough night.”

“Someone came to check on me earlier, and I'm sure they are going to check on me again later, I don't want them to come in and find us.” I said.

“I locked your door and mine. They won't knock on my door, but if they come back up here they can't get in. It will be fine, honey. But if you really want to sleep alone, I will leave.”

“No, please don't leave me alone.”

THE REST OF THE winter break went by fast, Kaisen left a week before Harper and I had to return to school for our final semester of high school. Guin-Bock doesn't usually interfere with the plans of the other rulers of Andeka, but Bala has been a worldwide threat. Guin-Bock set up a search for all the hospitals in Andeka and he informed the Government in the surrounding European countries. David said that if I shot Bala in the right place, it might take him months for him to heal if he doesn't have proper medical attention.

Chapter 16

As I stood on stage waiting for my name to be called I looked out into the audience searching for my Dad and Marilyn. They were sitting in the third row on the left side of the large auditorium. "Charlotte Callaway," the principal said. I walked across the stage, took the diploma from his left hand and shook his right, pausing to look out for pictures. I can't believe I was graduating already. The school year had flown by and I would soon be starting college. I was accepted into five colleges but am still unsure which one I will attend. I waited for everyone else to take their turn receiving their diplomas and when everyone was finished, the principal congratulated everyone and wished us good luck in the future.

"Congratulations! I am so proud of both of you." Marilyn sobbed as she hugged both Harper and I. I looked around, hoping that Kaisen had shown up early to surprise us but there was no sign of him. He promised me he would come to the house, where the reception was held after commencement, but wasn't going to be able to come early because of classes. I was just glad I would see him soon. I talked to him on the phone almost every day and we emailed all the time. I haven't seen him in five months, since Christmas break. I hoped to get some alone time with him before he had to go back in three days. He was able to stay that long only because he didn't have class on Monday. I hated it when I had to tell him goodbye, I hated being away from him for so long. I want so badly to go to the same college, but didn't apply because the waiting list for acceptance was a couple years long. Kaisen and Harper have been on the waiting list since they started kindergarten. This was no ordinary college though; it was Andeka University and specialized in each Cigam's individual abilities as well as learning to make a career with your talents in either world. It is the most prestigious college in all of Andeka. The tuition was incredibly high, but Dad and Marilyn had plenty of money saved up for all of us. I had been accepted to two Andeka Colleges and was interested in finding how to use my Shaire talent to its highest ability, but didn't know how that would help me with a career. Kaisen was automatically accepted into all Andeka Schools since he is leading heir to the Cigam-Bain throne. I wondered if that made a difference for me, too, since I was a direct descendant of Guin-Bock and I was in line for my own if I wanted it. I would have to ask Marilyn or Dad, but I think I do want his kingdom. I won't have to rule until I'm much older and married. If I start Andeka University I can be with Kaisen and Harper during school and I can get the best education about my powers. When applying for colleges last year I wasn't interested in going to Andeka University, I wasn't interested in college here at all, but Dad insisted I keep my options open. I wanted to go back to America and attend school there, but now that I know about the Cigam and my potential, I wanted to stay here and figure out how far I could really go.

I watched the door closely for Kaisen to arrive. Many people came and went, most of them I didn't even know, but I was bound to have that seeing as Harper and I were sharing a reception and I had only lived here for a year. I did recognize an older couple that walked in. I hadn't seen Charles or Gretta since I met Harper and Kaisen, they had sent me a Christmas present and I called to thank them, but they didn't come to visit often, and with Bala King a threat, they kept their distance.

"Thank you for coming," I said as Gretta hugged me.

"Congratulations Charlotte, you have turned in to a very special and talented young woman." She smiled.

"I don't think I thanked you for the emerald crystal ring. I really love it." I said as I looked down at where the ring sat on the ring finger on my right hand.

"I am glad you like it and I'm glad it has helped." She said as she picked up my hand to examine it. "I see you have a red crystal as well." She touched the bracelet that Kaisen had given me. "No wonder you are so talented. How long have you had this?"

"Since Christmas." I said not sure if I should tell her Kaisen gave it to me.

"I would say that you are quite lucky, but luck has nothing to do with it. I can predict your potential and you could be on the track to becoming a very powerful Cigam. I think you underestimate how special you really are, Charlotte." She laughed like she knew something I didn't. "Keep those crystals safe, it's not common for a single Cigam to have more than one kind."

"I will, I promise. But what did you mean, you can predict my potential?"

"I am a Cigam-Quaro: predictability of thoughts and actions. I can see what talents you possess."

"I am a Shaire, like my father." I told her.

"I know, but some Cigam Shaire don't get as powerful as others. You will be very powerful in your future, Charlotte, buy you must always follow your heart."

"You should take a trip to Youffe Castle in Brevil, and talk with Guin-Bock. He will tell you your destiny in the Cigam world. You will do great things." She smiled at me and handed me an envelope. "This should help get you there. Enjoy and Congratulations. And give Kaisen a kiss for me." She winked at me before she left to find where Charles had gone. I was a little scared to think she knew about Kaisen and I. I hope she wasn't going to say anything to anyone. I looked down at the envelope but with people coming in and out so much I didn't have enough time to open the gift. I pushed it into my pocket when I saw Marilyn walking my way.

"Kaisen is almost here, he just called. I bet you miss him a lot, I know I do and you kids have become so close since you moved here. I am so glad. What did Gretta have to say?" Marilyn asked.

"She gave me this." I said showing her the envelope. "She said I need to go to Brevil to meet Guin-Bock because he needs to tell me my destiny. Am I allowed to do that? Isn't he like a God or something?" I asked.

Marilyn laughed, "Some people see him as a God; he is the most powerful Cigam that ever lived. If David or a Cigam ruler accompanies you, you are more than welcome at Youffe Castle." She glanced up at some people that walked into the front door. "Oh, there are the Trechners, I need to go say hello." I watched as she walked over to a family that was talking with Harper. It was Lex and Luica's family. Luica was beautiful and if she wasn't planning to marry Kaisen, I might actually like her more. She was very nice to me, probably because she didn't know I loved Kaisen.

"Congratulations graduate!" The voice behind me made my heart skip a beat. Kaisen was smiling at me when I turned around.

"Kaisen!" I exclaimed. I couldn't contain my joy; I threw my arms around his neck to hug him. "I missed you so much."

"I missed you too," he laughed wrapping his arms around me too. Before he could let go, Harper was by our side and wrapped his arms around both of us. "I can't believe your graduated, Harper. Congratulations."

"Thanks, I'm just glad you could make it. It's been too long, but in a few months I'll be at A.U. with you." Harper said as he dropped his arms and stepped back. "Now all we have to do is get Charlotte in and we will be set."

"You two are such trouble makers, I'm not sure if I can handle college with you guys." I joked.

"Well who is going to get us out of trouble if you aren't there?" Harper asked.

"Good question. I've saved your life… how many times?" I laughed.

"At least two, if you don't count the time you wrote my paper for Early Civilization class. That A helped me pass and I'm pretty sure if I hadn't passed Mom would have murdered me."

"So then did you apply to A.U.?" Kaisen asked.

"No, there is a two year waiting list for acceptance; you guys will be done before I get the chance for someone to look at my application. I think I might go to the Cigam College in Franz, but I'm not sure yet."

"Don't be ridiculous, just tell David you want to go to A.U., he can probably pull some strings and get you in. Besides, CiCo is too far away." Kaisen said.

"And you don't want to be a CiCo do you?" Harper joked.

"Okay, I'll talk to my dad."

"So, what are the plans for tonight, anything fun?" Kaisen asked.

"Yeah there is a bonfire at the usual place; all the Graduates are going to be there. I'm sure they wouldn't mind if we brought you along though." Harper answered.

"Harper, come here." Harriett called from across the room over by the refreshment table.

Once he walked away, Kaisen said, "Do you think anyone would mind if I steal you away for a few minutes. It won't take long I promise."

"I think that would be fine, where are we going?" I asked. Kaisen smiled and walked out the door, I followed him down the hall to Marilyn's office. He shut the door behind us. I threw my arms around his neck and pulled him in for a kiss. He wrapped his arms around my waist and lifted me up and set me on top of Marilyn's desk. He dropped his arms and pushed me away.

"Happy Birthday, late." He said as he pulled out one small box from each of his pockets. He handed me the black one first. I knew what was in each of the boxes; it was the same thing he always got me. I opened the box and found a silver key shaped charm for my bracelet.

I smiled and was about to thank him but he cut me off before I could. "Open the next one. This one is a graduation present." He handed me the white box. This charm was a purple daisy, my class flower. He took the two charms and placed them on my bracelet next to my other two charms. He spaced them evenly so it looked balanced.

"Thank you. I love them." I said, staring into his gorgeous brown eyes.

"Good." He bent down to give me a short kiss. "Well we should probably get back to your party."

"Do we have to?" I tried to give him a mischievous grin. He smiled his gorgeous seductive smile at me that made me want to melt.

"You're going to get me in trouble aren't you?" He leaned down and kissed me again.

"Maybe." I mumbled between kisses. My arms were around his neck again and his arms had found my waist. Kaisen leaned over me then picked me up off the desk while keeping our lips locked. He gently set me on my feet and pulled away from me.

"I love you." He said.

"I love you, too." I smiled. He took my hand and kissed it before he dropped it and opened the door. We walked silently back to the reception.

The reception felt like it lasted forever. I went up to my room when it was finally over and changed into something for the party tonight. We would be leaving after dinner, which was in a half an hour. Kaisen said that he had to talk to David and Marilyn about something very important before dinner, so he couldn't come spend time with me. I, kind of, felt like he was hiding something.

"Mom, David, can I talk to you two in private please?" Kaisen said.

"Is something wrong?" Marilyn asked.

"Nothing's wrong. I just need to talk to you." They went to sit in the living room, away from everyone else. "Alright, well I wanted to talk to you about Luica. Now that Harper and I are out of school we don't need a backup plan if something happens to you, mom. And we have David now if something does happen. I have barely hung out with Luica and she still has a year left of school. I don't want to marry her."

"Kaisen, where did this come from? You never had a problem with this before." David asked.

"I know, but well I'm in love with someone else and I don't think it would fair to marry someone I don't love." He tried to explain.

"Kaisen, we did this for the kingdom, so that you would have another powerful family to rule with." Marilyn said.

"But this girl's family is probably just as powerful if not more and… please, is there any way to cancel it? I promise I won't screw this up."

"Kaisen, it's not that easy to just cancel an arranged marriage that has been planned for so long." Marilyn said.

"Hon, it's fine, we will work it out." David said to Marilyn. "Kaisen, how long have you known this girl?"

"I met her last year."

"And, does she love you back?"

"Yes, very much."

"I'll make you a deal." David told him. "I'm not going to cancel the marriage yet. It took too much effort to get it set up. But in a year, when Luica graduates and you guys get ready to start dating, if you and this other girl are set on being together, I will help you tell Luica's parents. You have to be one hundred percent sure this is who you are willing to spend the rest of your life with though. Kaisen this is a huge decision, not just for you but for Andeka, as well."

"I know, and thank you." Kaisen said hugging David and Marilyn.

"Don't tell anyone you plan to cancel the marriage, or that you are in a relationship with someone else." David said. "We don't want to start anything with Luica's family."

"I promise I won't."

"Well, I'm happy for you, son. I hope she is the one." He said as he got up and left the room.

"Kaisen, who is she? And why didn't you tell me." Marilyn asked.

"I couldn't tell you because of Luica, and I am not home enough to talk about it, I guess."

"I figured if you were in love, you would have at least come to me."

"I'm sorry. I wanted to tell you, but I couldn't." Kaisen explained.

"Well, do I get to meet her? What is she like?"

"Mom, just trust me, I'll tell you about her when the time is right." He said.

"Kaisen, I already know of her, now tell me about her?" Marilyn asked.

I had seen David leave the living room; I thought that they were done talking, so I walked into the room to get my jacket that was on the back of the couch. I saw Marilyn and Kaisen still talking. I hoped I wasn't interrupting. Kaisen looked up at me and smiled his gorgeous smile. I smiled back at him. He is so beautiful. Marilyn gasped, like she had just had an epiphany. I knew right away what had happen, when I looked at her she was looking back and forth between us.

"Kaisen!" Marilyn stared. "Charlotte?"

"Mom, please. Don't tell David."

"When did this happen? How did this happen?" Marilyn was shocked.

"I knew the minute I saw her. I can't help the way I feel, mom. I love her."

CPSIA information can be obtained at www.ICGtesting.com
Printed in the USA
LVOW080218261012

304533LV00001B/3/P